SOMETHING
Beautiful

ALSO BY JAMIE MCGUIRE

THE PROVIDENCE SERIES

Providence
Requiem
Eden
Sins of the Innocent: A Novella

THE BEAUTIFUL SERIES

Beautiful Disaster
Walking Disaster
A Beautiful Wedding: A Novella

THE MADDOX BROTHERS BOOKS

Beautiful Oblivion
Beautiful Redemption
Beautiful Sacrifice

Apolonia

Red Hill
Among Monsters: A Novella

Happenstance: A Novella Series (Books 1-3)

SOMETHING
Beautiful

JAMIE McGUIRE

To my sweet friend,
Megan Davis.
Thank you for you.

CONTENTS

PROLOGUE

Shepley

"QUIT BEING A PUSSY," Travis said, punching me in the arm.

I frowned and peered around us to see who had heard. Most of my fellow freshmen were within earshot, passing us to head into the cafeteria of Eastern State University for orientation. I recognized several faces from Eakins High, but there were even more I didn't recognize, like the two girls walking in together—one with a cardigan and a light-brown braid, the other with golden beach waves and short shorts. She glanced in my direction for half a second and then continued on, as if I were an inanimate object.

Travis held up his hands, a thick black leather cuff on his left wrist. I wanted to snatch it off and slap him with it.

"Sorry, Shepley Maddox!" he yelled my name as he looked around, sounding more like a robot or a really bad actor. Leaning in, he whispered, "I forgot I'm not supposed to call you that anymore—or at least, not on campus."

"Or anywhere, douche. Why'd you even come if you're going to be a dick?" I asked.

With his knuckles, Travis tapped the underside of the brim of my ball cap, almost knocking it off before I grabbed it. "I remember freshman orientation. I can't believe it's been a year. That's fucking weird." Pulling a lighter from his pocket, he lit a cigarette and blew out a puff of gray smoke.

A couple of girls hovering nearby swooned, and I tried not to vomit in my mouth.

"You're fucking weird. Thanks for showing me where to go. Now, get outta here."

"Hey, Travis," a girl said from the end of the sidewalk.

Travis nodded at her and then elbowed me, hard. "Later, cousin. While you're listening to boring shit, I'm going to be balls-deep in that brunette."

Travis greeted the girl, whoever she was. I had seen her in a few campus basements the year before when I came with Travis to his fights at The Circle, but I didn't know her name. I could watch her interact with Travis and learn everything I needed to know. She was already conquered.

Travis's weekly count had slowed down a little since his own freshman year but not by much. He hadn't said it out loud, but I could tell he was bored with the lack of challenge from the coeds. I was just looking forward to meeting a girl he hadn't bent over our couch.

The heavy door needed more than just a tug, and then I stepped inside, feeling the instant relief of air-conditioning. Rectangular tables pushed together, end over end, made five lines, separated strategically in areas for flow and access to the food line and salad bar. One lone circular table stood in a corner, and there sat the blonde with her friend and a flamboyant fellow with a bleach-blond faux hawk that seemed to have slammed into a wall at his hairline.

Darius Washington was sitting at the end of the line of tables, sufficiently close to the round table, so I waited for him to see me. Once he looked over, he waved like I'd hoped, and I joined him, pretty stoked that I was less than ten feet from the blonde. I didn't look back. Travis was an arrogant ass more often than not, but being around him meant free lessons on getting a girl's attention.

Lesson number one: Chase, but don't run.

Darius waved to the people seated at the round table.

I nodded at him. "Do you know them?"

He shook his head. "Just Finch. I met him yesterday when I moved into the dorms. He's hilarious."

"What about the girls?"

"No, but they're hot. Both of them."

"I need an introduction with the blonde."

"Finch seems to be friends with her. They've been talking since they sat down. I'll see what I can do."

I laid a firm hand on his shoulder, peeking back. She met my eyes, smiled, and looked away.

Be cool, Shep. Don't blow it.

Waiting for something as extremely boring as orientation to be over was made even worse by the anticipation of meeting that girl. Once in a while, I could hear her giggle. I promised myself I wouldn't look back, but I repeatedly failed. She was gorgeous with huge green eyes and wavy long hair, like she'd just been in the ocean and let it air-dry in the sun. The harder I listened for her voice, the more ridiculous I felt, but there was something about her, even since that first glance, that had me planning ways to impress her or to make her laugh. I'd do anything to get her attention, even for five minutes.

Once we were given our packets, and the campus layout, meal plans, and rules were explained ad nauseam, the Dean of Students, Mr. Johnson, dismissed us.

"Wait till we're outside," I said.

Darius nodded. "Don't worry. I got you. Just like the old days."

"In the old days, we chased high school girls. She is definitely not a high school girl. Probably not even when she was in high school," I said, following Darius out. "She's confident. She looks experienced, too."

"Nah, man. She looks like a good girl to me."

"Not that kind of experienced," I snarled.

Darius chuckled. "Calm down. You haven't even met her. You need to be careful. Remember Anya? You got all tangled up with her, and we thought you were going to die."

"Hey, fucker," Travis said from under a shady tree, about a hundred yards from the entrance. He blew out a last puff of smoke and pinched off the cherry, mashing it into the ground with his boot. He had the satisfied smile of a man post-orgasm.

"How?" I said in disbelief.

"Her dorm room is over there," he said, nodding his head toward Morgan Hall.

"Darius is going to introduce me to a girl," I said. "Just … keep your mouth shut."

Travis arched a brow and then nodded once. "Yes, dear."

"I mean it," I said, eyeing him. I shoved my hands in my jeans pockets and took a deep breath, watching Darius make small talk with Finch.

The brunette had already left, but thankfully, her friend seemed to be interested in sticking around.

"Stop fidgeting," Travis said. "You look like you're about to piss your pants."

"Shut up," I hissed.

Darius pointed in my direction, and Finch and the blonde looked at Travis and me.

"Fuck," I said, looking to my cousin. "Talk to me. We look like stalkers."

"You're dreamy," Travis said. "It's going to be love at first sight."

"Are they ... are they walking over?" I asked. My heart felt like it was about to claw through my rib cage, and I had the sudden urge to beat Travis's ass for being so flippant.

Travis scanned with his peripheral vision. "Yeah."

"Yeah?" I said, trying to suppress a smile. A stream of sweat escaped my hairline, and I quickly wiped it away.

Travis shook his head. "I'm going to kick you in the balls. You're already freaking out about this girl, and you haven't even met her yet."

"Hey," Darius said.

I turned and caught the hand he held out to me in a half high five and half handshake.

"This is Finch," Darius said. "He lives next door to me."

"Hi," Finch said, shaking my hand with a flirtatious smile.

"I'm America," the blonde said, holding out her hand to me. "Orientation was brutal. Thank God we're only freshmen once."

She was even more beautiful up close. Her eyes sparkled, her hair glowed in the sunlight, and her long legs looked like heaven in those frayed white shorts. She was almost as tall as me, even in sandals, and the way she held her mouth when she spoke, coupled with her full lips, was sexy as hell.

I took her hand and shook it once. "America?"

She smirked. "Go ahead. Make a dirty joke. I've heard them all."

"Have you heard, 'I'd love to fuck you for liberty'?" Travis asked.

I elbowed him, trying to keep a straight face.

America noticed my gesture. "Yes, actually."

"So ... are you accepting my offer?" Travis teased.

"No," America said without hesitation.

Yes. She's perfect.

"What about my cousin?" Travis asked, shoving me so hard that I had to sidestep.

"C'mon," I said, almost begging. "Excuse him," I said to America. "We don't let him out much."

"I can see why. Is he really your cousin?"

"I try not to tell people, but yes."

She scanned Travis and then turned her attention back to me. "So, are you going to tell me your name?"

"Shepley. Maddox," I added as an afterthought.

"What are you doing for dinner, Shepley?"

"What am *I* doing for dinner?" I asked.

Travis nudged me with his arm.

I shoved him off me. "Fuck off!"

America giggled. "Yes, you. I'm definitely not asking your cousin on a date."

"Why not?" Travis asked, feigning insult.

"Because I don't date toddlers."

Darius cackled, and Travis smiled, unfazed. He was being a dick on purpose to make me look like Prince Charming. The perfect wingman.

"Do you have a car?" she asked.

"I do," I said.

"Pick me up in front of Morgan Hall at six."

"Yeah … yeah, I can do that. See you then," I said.

She was already saying good-bye to Finch and walking away.

"Holy shit," I breathed. "I think I'm in love."

Travis sighed, and with a slap, he gripped the back of my neck. "Of course you do. Let's go."

America

Freshly cut grass, asphalt baking in the sun, and exhaust fumes—those were the smells that would remind me of the moment Shepley Maddox stepped out of his black vintage Charger and jogged up the steps of Morgan Hall to where I stood.

His eyes scanned over my pale blue maxi dress, and he smiled. "You look great. No, better than great. You look like I'd better bring my A game."

"You look average," I said, noting his polo and what were likely his dress jeans. I leaned in. "But you smell amazing."

His cheeks flushed dark enough to show through his bronze skin, and he offered a knowing smile. "I've been told I look average. It won't deter me from having dinner with you."

"You have?"

He nodded.

"They were lying. Just like me." I passed him, heading down the steps.

Shepley hurried past me, reaching the door handle of the passenger side before I could. He tugged on it, opening the door wide in one motion.

"Thank you," I said, sitting in the passenger seat.

The leather felt cool against my skin. The interior had been freshly vacuumed and polished, and it smelled like generic air freshener.

When he sat in his seat and turned to me, I couldn't help but smile. His enthusiasm was adorable. Kansas boys weren't so … eager.

By the golden tone of his skin and his solid arm muscles that bulged every time he moved them, I decided he must have worked outside all summer—maybe baling hay or loading something heavy. His hazel-green eyes practically glowed, and his dark hair—although not as short as Travis's—had been lightened by the sun, reminding me of Abby's warm caramel color.

"I was going to take you to the Italian place here in town, but it's cooled off enough outside to … I … I just wanted to hang out and get to know you instead of being interrupted by a waiter. So, I did that," he said, nodding to the backseat. "I hope it's okay."

I tensed, turning slowly to see what he was talking about. In the middle of the bench seat, secured with a seat belt, was a covered woven basket sitting on a thickly folded blanket.

"A picnic?" I said, unable to hide the surprise and delight in my voice.

He breathed out, relieved. "Yeah. Is that okay?"

I flipped around in the seat, bouncing once as I faced forward. "We'll see."

Shepley drove us to a private pasture just south of town. He parked in a narrow gravel drive and stepped out just long enough to unlock the gate and push it open. The Charger's engine growled as he drove down two parallel lines of bare ground amid the acres of tall grass.

"You've worn down a path, huh?"

"This land belongs to my grandparents. There's a pond at the bottom where Travis and I used to go fishing all the time."

"Used to?"

He shrugged. "We're the youngest grandkids. We lost both sets of grandparents by the time we were in middle school. Besides being busy with sports and classes in high school, it just felt wrong to fish out here without Papa."

"I'm sorry," I said. I still had all my grandparents, and I couldn't imagine losing any of them. "Both sets? You mean, all three sets?" I said, wondering aloud. "Oh God, I'm sorry. That was rude."

"No, no … it's a valid question. I get that a lot. We're double cousins. Our dads are brothers, and our moms are sisters. I know. Weird, huh?"

"No, that's pretty great actually."

After we cleared a small hill, Shepley parked the Charger under a shady tree ten yards from a five-ish-acre pond. The summer heat had helped grow the cattails and lily pads, and the water was beautiful, wrinkling in the light breeze.

Shepley opened my door, and I stepped out onto freshly mowed grass. As I looked around, he ducked into the backseat, reappearing with the basket and a quilt. His arms were free of any tattoos, also unlike his heavily inked cousin. I wondered if there were any under his shirt. Then I had the sudden urge to remove his clothes to find the answer.

He spread the multicolored quilt with one flick, and it fell perfectly to the ground.

"What?" he asked. "Is it—"

"No, this is amazing. I'm just … that quilt is so beautiful. I don't think I should sit on it. It looks brand-new." The fabric was still crisp and bore creases where it had been folded.

Shepley puffed out his chest. "My mom made it. She's made dozens. She made this for me when I graduated. It's a replica." His cheeks flushed.

"Of what?"

As soon as I asked the question, he winced.

I tried not to smile. "It's a bigger version of your childhood blankie, isn't it?"

He closed his eyes and nodded. "Yeah."

I sat down on the quilt and crossed my legs, patting the space beside me. "C'mere."

"I'm not sure I can. I think I just died of embarrassment."

I looked up at him, squinting one eye from the beam of sunlight escaping through the tree leaves above. "I have a blankie, too. Murfin is in my dorm room——under my pillow."

His shoulders relaxed, and he sat down, placing the basket in front of him. "Blake."

"Blake?"

"I guess I tried to say 'blank,' and it turned into Blake along the way."

I smiled. "I like that you didn't lie."

He shrugged, still embarrassed. "I'm not very good at it anyway."

I leaned in, nudging his shoulder with mine. "I like that, too."

Shepley beamed and then opened the basket, pulling out a covered plate of cheese and crackers and then a bottle of zinfandel and two plastic champagne flutes.

I stifled a laugh, and Shepley chuckled.

"What?" he asked.

"It's just … this is the cutest date I've ever been on."

He poured the zin. "Is that a good thing?"

I spread Brie on a cracker and took a bite, nodding, and then a little sip of wine to wash it down. "You definitely get an A for effort."

"Good. I don't want it to be so cute that I'll be friend-zoned," he said, almost to himself.

I licked the cracker and wine from my lips, looking at his. The air between us changed. It was heavier … electric. I leaned toward him, and he made a failed attempt to hide the surprise and excitement in his eyes.

"Can I kiss you?" I asked.

His eyebrows shot up. "You wanna … you wanna kiss me?" He looked around. "Right now?"

"Why not?"

Shepley blinked. "I've just, um … never had a girl …"

"Am I making you uncomfortable?"

He quickly shook his head. "Definitely not what I'm feeling right now."

He cupped my cheek and pulled me in without a second hesitation. I immediately opened my mouth, tasting the wetness of the inside of his lips. His tongue was soft and warm and tasted like sweet mint.

I hummed, and he pulled away.

"Let's, um … I made sandwiches. Do you like ham or turkey?"

I touched my lips, smiling, and then forced a straight face. Shepley looked positively flustered in the best possible way. He handed me a wax paper–wrapped square, and I carefully pinched a corner, pulling until I saw white bread.

"Thank God," I said. "White bread is the best!"

"I know, right? I can't stand whole wheat."

"Bleach and calories be damned!"

I peeled open the paper and tasted the carefully crafted turkey and Swiss with what smelled like chipotle ranch and lettuce and tomato. I looked up at Shepley, horrified. "Oh God."

He stopped chewing and swallowed. "What?"

"Tomatoes?"

His eyes filled with horror. "Fuck. Are you allergic?" He frantically looked around. "Do you have an EpiPen? Should I take you to the hospital?"

I fell backward, gasping and clutching at my throat.

Shepley hovered over me, not sure where to touch me or how to help. "Fuck. Fuck! What do I do?"

I grabbed his shirt and pulled him down to me, concentrating on speaking. Finally, the words came. "Mouth-to-mouth," I whispered.

Shepley tensed, and then all his muscles relaxed. "You're messing with me?"

He sat up as I burst into laughter.

"Jesus, Mare, I was freaking out!"

My giggling faded, and I smiled at him. "My best friend calls me Mare."

He sighed. "I am so going to get friend-zoned."

I raised my hand above my head, twirling strands of my long hair, feeling the cool grass beneath my arm. "Better head that off with aggressive affection."

He raised an eyebrow. "I'm not sure I can handle you."

"You won't know unless you try."

Shepley anchored himself with his arms on each side of me, and then he leaned down, touching his lips to mine. I reached down, bunching my skirt, and smiled as the hem rose above my knees. His lips worked against mine as he positioned himself between my legs in one smooth motion.

His hands felt so good on my skin, and my hips rolled and shifted in reaction. He hooked his hand behind my knee, pulling it to his hip.

"Holy shit," he said against my lips.

I pulled him closer. The hardness behind his zipper pressed against me, and I hummed, feeling the denim on my fingertips as I unbuttoned his jeans.

When I reached inside, Shepley froze. "I didn't bring a ... I wasn't expecting this. At all."

With my free hand, I fished a small packet from the side of my strapless bra. "Wishing for one of these?"

Shepley looked down at the foil square in my hand, and his expression changed. He sat back on his knees, watching me, as I pushed myself up with my elbows.

"Let me guess," I said, tasting the acidity in my words. "We just met. I'm sexually forward, and I brought a condom, so that must mean I'm a whore, making you wholly uninterested."

He frowned.

"Say it. Say what you're thinking," I said, daring him. "Give it to me in real time. I can take it."

"This girl is articulate and fun and quite possibly the most beautiful creature I've ever seen in real life. How in God's name did I manage to be in this moment with her?" He leaned forward, half-confused, half in awe. "And I'm not sure if this is a test." He looked down at my lips. "Because, trust me, if it is, I want to pass."

I smiled and brought him in for another kiss. He tilted his head, eagerly leaning in.

I held him at bay, just inches from my mouth. "I might be fast, but I like to be kissed slow."

"I can do that."

Shepley's lips were full and soft. He had an air of nervousness and inexperience, but the way he kissed me told a different story. He pecked my mouth once, lingering for a bit, before pulling away, and then he kissed me again.

"Is it true?" he whispered. "That fast girls don't usually stick around for long?"

"That's the thing about being fast. You don't know what you'll do until you do it."

He exhaled. "Just grant me a favor," he said between kisses. "When you're ready to walk away, try to let me down easy."

"You first," I whispered.

He laid me back onto the blanket, finishing what I'd started.

CHAPTER ONE

Shepley

AMERICA LOOKED LIKE AN ANGEL, pressing the phone to her ear, tears glistening down her face. Even if they weren't happy tears, she was still nothing less than beautiful.

She tapped the screen and held her cell in the space between her crisscrossed legs. The thick hot-pink case lay on the bed of her elegant fingers and long olive-green skirt, reminding me of our first date—which happened to be the first day we'd met ... along with a few other firsts. I'd loved her then, but I loved her even more now, seven months and one breakup later, even with smudged mascara and bloodshot eyes.

"They're married." America breathed out a laugh and wiped her nose.

"I heard. I guess the Honda is at the airport then? I can drop you off and follow you back to the apartment. When does their flight get in?"

She sniffed, getting flustered with herself. "Why am I crying? What is wrong with me? I'm not even surprised. Nothing they do surprises me anymore!"

"Two days ago, we thought they were dead. Now, Abby is Travis's wife ... and you just met my parents for the first time. It's been a big weekend, baby. Don't beat yourself up."

I touched her hand, and she seemed to relax, but it didn't last for long before she bristled.

"You're related to her," she said. "I'm just the friend. Everyone is related but me. I'm an outsider."

I hooked my arm around her neck and pulled her into my chest, kissing her hair. "You'll be part of the family soon enough."

She pushed me away, another bothersome thought floating around in her pretty little head. "They're newlyweds, Shep."

"So?"

"Think about it. They're not going to want a roommate."

My eyebrows pulled in. *What the hell am I going to do?*

As soon as the answer popped into my mind, I smiled. "Mare."

"Yeah?"

"We should get an apartment."

She shook her head. "We've talked about this."

"I know. I want to talk about it again. Travis and Abby eloping is the perfect excuse."

"Really?"

I nodded.

I watched patiently while the possibilities swam behind her eyes, the corners of her mouth curling up more every second.

"It's exciting to think about, but in reality—"

"It'll be perfect," I said.

"Deana will hate me even more."

"My mom doesn't hate you."

She eyed me, dubious. "Are you sure?"

"I know my mom. She likes you. A lot."

"Then let's do it."

I sat in disbelief for a moment and then reached for her. It was already surreal—the fact that, all weekend, she had been in the home where I'd grown up, and now, she was sitting on my bed. Since the day we'd met, I'd felt like reality had been altered. Miracles like America just didn't happen to me. Not only had my past and unbelievable present intertwined, but America Mason had just agreed to take the next step with me. Calling it a *big weekend* would be an understatement.

"I'm going to have to find a job," I said, trying to catch my breath. "I have a little money saved up from fights, but considering the fire, I don't see any fights happening anytime soon, if ever again."

America shook her head. "I wouldn't want you to go anyway, not after the other night. It's too dangerous, Shep. We're going to be attending funerals for weeks."

Like a bomb, her words blew away all the excitement from our discussion.

"I don't want to think about it."

"Don't you have a house meeting tomorrow?"

I nodded. "We're going to raise money for the families and do something at the house in honor of Derek, Spencer, and Royce. I still can't believe they're gone. It hasn't hit me yet, I guess."

America chewed on her lip and then put her hand on mine. "I'm so glad you weren't there." She shook her head. "It might be selfish, but it's all I can think about."

"It's not selfish. I've thought the same thing about you. If Dad hadn't insisted I bring you home this week … we could have been there, Mare."

"But we weren't. We're here. Travis and Abby eloped, and we're moving in together. I want to think happy thoughts."

I began to ask a question but hesitated.

"What?"

I shook my head.

"Say it."

"You know how Travis and Abby are. What if they split up? Where would that leave you and me?"

"Probably letting one of them crash on our couch and listening to them argue in our living room until they got back together."

"You think they'll stay together?"

"I think it'll be rocky for a while. They're … volatile. But Abby's different with Travis, and he's definitely different with her. I think they need each other in, like, the most genuine way. You know what I mean?"

I smiled. "I do."

She looked around my room, her eyes pausing on my baseball trophies and a picture of my cousins and me when I was around eleven.

"Did they just kick your ass all the time?" she asked. "You were the little cousin of the Maddox brothers. That had to be just … crazy."

"No," I said simply. "We were more like brothers than cousins. I was the youngest, so they protected me. Thomas sort of babied Travis and me. Travis always got us in trouble, and it would be his ass. I was the peacekeeper, I guess, always petitioning for mercy." I laughed at the memories.

"I'm going to have to ask your mom about that sometime."

"About what?"

"How she and Diane ended up with Jack and Jim."

"Dad claims it happened with much finesse," I said, chuckling. "Mom says it was a train wreck."

"Sounds like us—Travis and Abby, and you and me." Her eyes sparkled.

Almost a year after I'd moved out, my bedroom was almost the same. My old computer was still gathering dust on the small wooden desk in the corner, the same books were on the shelves, and two awkward prom photos were kept in cheap frames on the nightstand. The only missing items were pictures and framed newspaper clippings of my football days that used to hang on the gray walls. High school felt like a lifetime ago. Any life without America felt like an alternate universe. Both the fire and Travis getting married had somehow solidified my feelings for America even more.

A warmth came over me that only happened when she was around. "So, I guess that means we're next," I said without thinking.

"Next for what?" Recognition pushed her eyebrows to her hairline, and she stood. "Shepley Walker Maddox, you just keep your diamonds to yourself. I am not anywhere near ready for that. Let's just play house and be happy, mmkay?"

"Okay," I said, holding up my hands. "I didn't mean soon. I just said next."

She sat. "Okay. Just so we're clear, I have Travis and Abby's second wedding to plan, and I don't have time for another one."

"Second wedding?"

"She owes me. We made a promise a long time ago that we would be each other's maid of honor. She is going to have a real bachelorette party and a real wedding, and she is going to let me plan it. All of it. It's mine," she said, not even a hint of a smile on her lips.

"Understood."

She threw her arms around my neck, her hair smothering me. I buried my face deeper into her golden locks, welcoming suffocation if it meant I was close to her.

"Your room is really clean, and so is your room at the apartment," she whispered. "I'm not a clean freak."

"I know."

"You might get sick of me."

"Not possible."

"You'll love me forever?"

"Longer."

She squeezed me tight, breathing out a content sigh, the kind I worked my ass off for because it would make me so damn happy when she did it. Her sweet, happy sighs were like the first day of summer, like anything was possible, like it was my superpower.

"Shepley!" Mom called.

I leaned back and took America by the hand, leading her out of my room, down the hall, and into the downstairs living room. My parents were sitting there, together in their worn love seat, holding hands. That furniture was the first they'd ever bought together, and they refused to get rid of it. The rest of the house was full of contemporary leather and modern rustic design, but they would spend most of their time in the lower level, down the hall from my room, on the itchy blue floral fabric of their first love seat.

"We're going to have to run an errand soon, Mom. We'll be back in time for dinner."

"Where are you going?" she asked.

America and I traded glances.

"Abby just called. She wanted us to stop by the apartment for a little bit," America said.

She and Abby were well versed in off-the-cuff half-truths. I imagined Abby had taught America well after she moved to Wichita. They'd had to do a lot of sneaking around when they were making underage trips to Vegas, so Abby could gamble and help her loser dad get out of debt.

Dad scooted forward on his seat. "Think you could hold on for a minute? We need to ask you a few questions."

"I just have to get my purse," America said, gracefully excusing herself.

Mom smiled, but I frowned.

"What is this about?"

"Have a seat, son," Dad said, patting the arm of the brown leather recliner adjacent to their love seat.

"I like her," Mom said. "I really, really like her. She's confident and strong, and she loves you that way, too."

"I hope so," I said.

"She does," Mom said with a knowing smile.

"So ..." I began. "What do you need to tell me that you couldn't say in front of her?"

My parents looked at one another, and then Dad patted Mom's knee with his free hand.

"Is it bad?" I asked.

They struggled to find the words, answering without speaking.

"Okay. How bad is it?"

"Uncle Jim called," Dad said. "The police were over at the house last night, asking questions about Travis. They think he is responsible for the fight in Keaton Hall. Do you know anything about it?"

"You can tell us," Mom said.

"I know about the fight," I said. "It wasn't the first one. But Travis wasn't there. You were right here when I called him. He was at the apartment."

Dad shifted in his seat. "He's not at the apartment now. Do you know where he is? Abby is missing as well."

"Okay," I said simply. I didn't want to answer either way.

Dad saw right through me. "Where are they, son?"

"Travis hasn't talked to Uncle Jim yet, Dad. Don't you think we should give him a chance first?"

Dad considered that. "Shepley ... did you have anything to do with those fights?"

"I've been to some of them. Most of them this year."

"But not this one," Mom clarified.

"No, Mom, I was here."

"That's what we said to Jim," Dad said. "And that's what we'll tell the police if they ask."

"You didn't leave? At any point during the night?" Mom asked.

"No. I got a text about the fight, but this weekend was important to America. I didn't even respond."

Mom relaxed.

"When did Travis leave? And why?" Dad asked.

"Dad," I said, trying to remain patient, "Uncle Jim will tell you after Travis talks to him."

America peeked from my bedroom doorway, and I signaled for her to join us.

"We should go," she said.

I nodded.

"You'll be back for dinner?" Mom asked.

"Yes, ma'am," America said.

I dragged her up the stairs behind me to the main level and out the door.

"I looked up their flight," she said as we settled into the Charger. "Two more hours."

"Then we should roll into Chicago just in time."

America leaned over to kiss my cheek. "Travis could be in a lot of trouble, couldn't he?"

"Not if I can help it."

"*We*, baby. Not if we can help it."

I looked down into her eyes.

Travis had already cost me my relationship with America once. I loved him like a brother, but I wouldn't risk it again. I couldn't let America protect Travis and get in trouble with the authorities even if she wanted to.

"Mare, I love you for saying that, but I need you to stay out of this one."

She wrinkled her nose in disgust. "Wow."

"Travis will take a lot of people with him if he goes down for this. I don't want you to be one of them."

"Will you? Be one of them?"

"Yes," I said without hesitation. "But you were at my parents' all weekend. You know nothing. Understand?"

"Shep—"

"I mean it," I said. My voice was uncharacteristically stern, and she leaned back a bit. "Promise me."

"I ... can't promise you that. Abby is family. I'd do anything to protect her. By proxy, that includes Travis. We're all in this together, Shepley. Travis would do the same for me or for you, and you know it."

"That's different."

"Not at all. Not even a little bit."

I leaned down to kiss her damn stubborn lips that I loved so much, and I twisted the ignition, firing up the Charger. "They can just drive your car home."

"Oh, no," she said, glaring out the window. "The last time I let them borrow my car, they got married without me."

I chuckled.

"Drop me off at the Honda. I'll drive them home, and they're both going to hear it from me the entire way home. And Travis isn't getting out of it by riding with you either, so if he asks—"

I shook my head, amused. "I wouldn't dare."

CHAPTER TWO

America

I DABBED THE SWEAT beading above my top lip with the back of one hand, pressing down on the top of my wide-brimmed hat with the other. Across the palm trees and shrubs flowering in every bright color imaginable were Taylor and Falyn sitting together at a table at Bleuwater.

I removed my oversized black sunglasses and narrowed my eyes, watching them argue. The perfect island second wedding had taken most of the year to plan, and the Maddox boys were ruining it.

"Jesus," I sighed. "What now?"

Shepley grabbed my hand, looking in the same direction until he eyed the problem. "Oh. They don't look happy at all."

"Thomas and Liis are fighting, too. The only ones getting along are Trent and Cami, and Tyler and Ellie, but Ellie never gets mad."

"Tyler and Ellie aren't really … together," Shepley said.

"Why does everyone keep saying that? They're together. They're just not saying they're together."

"It's been that way for a long time, Mare."

"I know. Enough already."

Shepley pulled my back against his chest and nuzzled my neck. "You forgot us."

"Huh?"

"You forgot to say us. We're getting along."

I paused. Planning and organizing and making sure everything flowed smoothly had kept me busy. Aside from the reception at Sails, I'd barely seen Shepley. But he hadn't once complained.

I touched his cheek. "We always get along."

Shepley offered a half smile. "Travis has officially gotten married twice before the rest of us."

"Trenton isn't far behind."

"You don't know that."

"They're engaged, baby. I'm pretty sure."

"They haven't set a date."

I smoothed my sheer black cover-up and pulled Shepley toward the beach. "Do you not approve?"

He shrugged. "I don't know. It's weird. She dated Thomas first. You just don't do that."

"Well, she did. And if she hadn't, Trent wouldn't be so happy." I stopped at the edge of the sand, pointing to a small group of Maddoxes gathered at the water's edge.

Travis was sitting on a white plastic lounge chair, puffing on a cigarette and staring across the ocean. Trenton and Camille were standing a few feet away from him, watching him with concerned expressions.

My stomach sank. "Oh, no. Oh, fuck."

"I'm on it," Shepley said, letting go of my hand to walk toward Travis.

"Fix it. I don't care what you have to say or do … just fix it. They can't fight on their honeymoon."

Shepley waved back to me, letting me know that he had everything under control. His shoes flipped sand as he trudged to where his cousin sat. Travis looked devastated. I couldn't imagine what might have happened between marital bliss just the night before and this morning.

Shepley sat with his feet planted between his chair and Travis's, and he clasped his hands together. Travis didn't move. He didn't acknowledge Shepley. He just stared at the water.

"This is bad," I whispered.

"What's bad?" Abby asked, startling me. "Whoa. Jumpy this morning? What are you staring at? Where's Shep?" She stretched her neck to look past me at the beach.

"Fuck," she whispered. "That looks bad. Are you and Shepley fighting?"

I spun around. "No. Shepley went to find out what was wrong with Trav. You're not? Fighting, I mean?"

Abby shook her head. "No. Pretty sure that's not what anyone would call what he did to me all night. Wrestling maybe—"

"Did he say anything to you this morning?"

"He left before I woke up."

"Now, he ... he looks like that!" I said, pointing. "What the hell happened?"

"Why are you yelling?"

"I'm not yelling!" I took a breath. "I mean ... I'm sorry. Everyone's mad. I don't want angry people at this wedding. I want happy people."

"The wedding is over, Mare," Abby said, patting my backside, as she passed. She strolled out to the beach.

Marriage had made her confident, calmer, and slower to react when something was amiss. Abby had the security of knowing that if a problem stood before them, they would figure it out and be holding hands on the other side. Travis the Boyfriend had been unpredictable, but Travis the Husband was Abby's teammate, the only real family she had.

I could almost see triumph in the way she moved as she closed in on him and Shepley. Whatever was wrong, Abby was unafraid. Travis was unbeatable, just like her. They had nothing to fear.

That part of being married was appealing to me, but being married to a Maddox would be work, and I wasn't sure I was ready for that yet—even if my Maddox was Shepley.

The moment Abby knelt next to Travis, he threw his arms around her and buried his face in the crook of her neck. Shepley stood and took a few steps back, glancing at me for just a moment, before watching Abby work her magic.

"Good morning, sweet pea," Mom said, touching my shoulder.

I turned to hug her. "Hi. How did you sleep?"

Mom looked around and sighed. The lines on each side of her mouth deepened when she smiled. "This place, America. You did a really good job."

"Too good," Dad teased.

"Mark, stop," Mom said, nudging him with her elbow. "She's already said she's not in a hurry. Leave her alone." She looked at me. "Are we still on for brunch?"

"Yeah," I said, distracted by Travis hugging Abby on the beach. I chewed on my lip. At least they weren't fighting—or maybe they were making up.

"What is it?" Dad asked. He looked in the same direction I was, immediately seeing Travis and Abby. "Good God, they're not arguing, are they?"

"No. Everything is fine," I assured him.

"Travis didn't attack some drunken spring breaker for staring at his wife, did he?"

"No." I chuckled. "Travis is calmer … ish."

"Abby has the face, Pam," Dad said.

"No, she doesn't," I snapped back, more to myself than to him.

"You're right," Mom said. "That is definitely the face."

They meant Abby's poker face. Any stranger would think nothing of it, but we all knew what it meant.

I turned to them with a contrived smile. "I reserved a table for six. I think Jack and Deana are already heading that way. I'll just grab Shepley, and we'll meet you there."

Mom batted her eyes and pretended like she didn't know I was trying to get rid of them, just like all the times when they'd ignored Abby's poker face when we were getting caught in a lie. My parents weren't stupid, but they were also nontraditional in the way that, as long as we were safe, they'd allow us to make mistakes. They didn't know those mistakes had been made in Las Vegas.

"America," Mom said. Her tone alerted me to something more serious than the scene on the beach. "We have an idea on what this brunch is about."

"No, you don't," I began.

She held up her hand. "Before you make everyone at the table uncomfortable, your dad and I have discussed it, and our feelings haven't changed."

My mouth fell open, and my words tripped over my tongue several times before I could form a coherent sentence. "Mom, just please hear us out."

"You still have two years left," Mom said.

"It's a great apartment. It's close to campus—" I said.

"School has never come easy to you," Mom interjected.

"Shepley and I study all the time. I'm carrying a three-point-oh."

"Barely," Mom said, sadness in her eyes.

She hated telling me no, but she would when she felt it was important, which made it really hard for me to argue.

"Mom—"

"America, the answer is no." Dad shook his head, holding up his hands, palms out. "We're not financing an apartment with your boyfriend, and we don't feel like you could hold satisfactory grades and work enough hours to pay rent, even half the rent. We don't know how Shepley's parents feel, but we can't agree to it. Not yet."

My shoulders fell. For weeks, Shepley had been preparing a speech with calm rebuttals and sound arguments. He would be devastated—again—just like the last time when we'd announced that we would be moving in together and were shut down.

"Daddy," I whined, a last-ditch effort.

He wasn't moved. "Sorry, sweet pea. We'd appreciate it if you didn't bring it up at brunch. It's our last day. Let's just—"

"I get it. Okay," I said.

They both hugged me and then walked toward the restaurant. I pressed my lips together, trying to figure out a way to break the news to Shepley. Our plan had been sunk before we even had a chance to present it to our parents.

Shepley

"Shit," I said under my breath.

America's conversation with her parents hadn't looked pleasant, and when they walked off and she looked at me, I already knew what had happened.

"Trav, look at me," Abby said, holding his chin until his eyes focused on hers.

"I can't tell you. That's as truthful as I can be."

Abby put her hands on her hips and bit her lips together, scanning the horizon. "Can you at least tell me why you can't tell me?" She looked back at him with her big gray eyes.

"Thomas asked me not to, and if I do … we won't be able to be together."

"Just answer me this," Abby said. "Does it have to do with another woman?"

Confusion and then horror reflected in Travis's eyes, and he hugged her again. "Christ, baby, no. Why would you even ask that?"

Abby hugged him, resting her cheek on his shoulder. "If it's not someone else, then I trust you. I guess I just won't know."

"Really?" Travis asked.

"Travis, what the hell is it?" I asked.

Travis frowned at me.

"Shep," Abby said, "it's between Thomas and Travis."

I nodded. If he didn't tell Abby, he wasn't going to tell me. "Okay." I play-punched Travis's shoulder with the side of my fist. "You feel better? Abby's cool with it."

"I wouldn't say that," Abby said. "But I'll respect it. For now."

A cautious smile spread on Travis's face, and he held out his hand to his wife.

"Hey," America said. "Everything good here?"

"We're good," Abby said, smiling at Travis.

Travis simply nodded.

America looked to me, the ocean breeze blowing thick strands of her long blonde hair in her face. "Can we talk?"

My eyebrows pulled in, and she winced.

"Don't look at me like that," she said.

Travis and Abby walked down the beach, leaving us alone.

"I saw you with your parents. Looked like an intense conversation."

"It wasn't pleasant. They knew why we'd asked to have brunch with them and your parents. They asked me not to bring it up."

"You mean, moving in together?" I said, my entire body feeling tense.

"Yes."

"But … they haven't heard what we have to say. I have points."

"I know. But they're focused on my grades, and they don't feel like I'll be able to work and keep a three-point-oh."

"Baby, I'll help you."

"I know. But … they're right. If I don't have time to study, it won't matter how much you help me."

We had picked out an apartment. I'd already paid the money to hold it.

I frowned. "Okay, then I'll support us. I'll take a break from school if I have to."

"What? No! That's a terrible idea."

I gripped her tiny arms in both my hands. "Mare, we're adults. We can move in together if we want."

"My parents won't support me if I live with you. They said that, Shep. They won't help me with tuition or books and definitely not living expenses. They think it's the wrong decision."

"They're wrong."

"You're talking about quitting school. I'm thinking they're right."

My heart began to race. This felt like the beginning of the end. If America wasn't interested in moving in, maybe she was losing interest in me altogether.

"Marry me," I blurted out.

Her nose wrinkled. "Pardon?"

"They can't say anything if we're married."

"That won't change the facts. I'll still have to work, and my grades will suffer."

"I told you. I'll support us."

"By dropping out of school? No. That's stupid, Shep. Stop."

"If Travis and Abby can do it—"

"We're not Travis and Abby. We're definitely not going to get married to solve a problem like they did."

I felt my veins swell with anger, the pressure making the blood boil in my face and compress behind my eyes. I walked away from her, folding my hands on top of my head, willing the Maddox temper to wane. The waves were slapping on the shore, and I could hear Trenton and Camille talking from one direction, Travis and Abby from another.

Kids with their families along with young and old couples were beginning to filter down from their rooms. We were surrounded by people who had their shit together. America and I had been together for longer than Travis and Abby, and Trent and Camille. They were either married or engaged, and America and I couldn't even make it to the next step.

From behind me, America slipped her arms beneath mine, interlocking her fingers at my middle, pressing her cheek and tits against my back. I tilted my head toward the sky. I fucking loved it when she did that.

"There's no hurry, baby," she whispered. "It'll happen. We just need to be patient."

"So ... don't bring it up at brunch."

She wiggled, trying to shake her head against my back.

I exhaled a deep sigh. "Fuck."

CHAPTER THREE

America

"Happy anniversary to you," I sang, handing Abby a card and a small white box with a blue bow.

She looked at her watch and then wiped her eyes. "I liked our first anniversary much better."

"Probably because I planned it, we were in Saint Thomas, and everything was perfect."

Abby shot me a look.

"Or because Travis was actually present," I said, trying to keep the hate from my voice.

Travis had been traveling a lot for work, and although Abby seemed to understand, I certainly didn't. He was working part-time as a personal trainer after his classes, but at some point, the owner had asked him to travel for sales or … I wasn't quite sure. It was much better pay, but it was always at the last minute, and he never said no.

"Don't give me that look, Mare. He's on his way right now. He can't help it that his flight was delayed."

"He could have *not* traveled halfway across the country so close to your anniversary. Stop defending him. It's infuriating."

"For whom?"

"Me! The one who has to watch you cry over your anniversary card that he wrote before he left because he knew there was a good possibility he'd miss it. He should be here!"

Abby sniffed and sighed. "He didn't want to miss it, Mare. He is sick over it. Don't make it worse."

"Fine," I said. "But I'm not leaving you here alone. I'm staying until he gets here."

Abby hugged me, and I hooked my chin over her shoulder, glancing around the dim apartment. It looked so different from when I had first walked through the door our freshman year. Travis had insisted that Abby make the space her own after Shepley had moved out, shortly after they'd gotten married. Instead of street signs and beer posters, the walls were adorned with paintings, wedding pictures, and family pictures with Toto. There were lamps and tables and ceramic décor.

I turned back to look at the full plates of cold food on the small dining table. The candle had burned down to dried drippings of wax that nearly touched the reclaimed wood.

"Dinner smells good. I'll be sure to rub it in."

Shepley texted me, and I tapped out a quick reply.

"Shep?" Abby asked.

"Yeah. He thought I'd be home by now."

"How is that going?"

"He's a clean freak, Abby. How do you think it's going?" I said, disgusted.

"You were all mad when your parents said you couldn't move in with him. You both sulked in the dorms for a year and a half. They finally gave in, and now, you hate it."

"I don't hate it. I'm afraid he's going to hate me."

"It's been almost three years, Mare. If it were possible for Shepley to do anything but worship you, I doubt it would be over a pair of dirty socks."

I pulled my knees up to my chest, almost wishing it were him in my arms. I often wondered when being around Shepley or even thinking about him would stop making me feel so much, but the passing time had only made my feelings stronger.

"We graduate next summer, Abby. Can you believe it?"

"No. Then we really have to be adults."

"You've been an adult since you were a kid."

"True."

"I keep thinking he's going to ask me to marry him."

Abby arched her brow.

"If he says my name a certain way or we go to a fancy restaurant, I think it's going to be it, but he never does."

"He did ask you, Mare, remember? You said no. Twice."

I winced, remembering that morning on the beach and a few
months later with the candlelight glinting in his eyes, the
homemade pasta, and the supreme disappointment on his face.
"But that was last year."

"You think you missed your chance, don't you? You think he'll
never get up the nerve to ask you again." I didn't answer, but she
continued, "Why don't you ask him?"

"Because I know it's important to him that he ask me."

Proposing to Shepley had crossed my mind, but I remembered
what he'd said about the news that Abby had popped the question
to Travis. It had bothered him almost as much as the realization
that his feelings on the subject were so traditional. Shepley felt it
was his place as the man to ask. I hadn't realized that if I wasn't
ready when he proposed, he would stop asking.

"Do you want him to? Ask you again?"

"Of course I do. We don't have to get married right away,
right?"

"Right. So, what's your hurry to get engaged?" she asked.

"I don't know. He seems bored."

"Bored? With you? Didn't he just text to check on you?"

"Yes, but——"

"Are you bored?"

"*Bored* isn't the right word. He's uncomfortable. We're
stagnate, and I can tell it bothers him."

"Maybe he's waiting on a signal from you that you're ready?"

"I have been dropping them right and left, except for
mentioning America's Famous No. We have an unspoken
agreement to leave it unspoken."

"Maybe you should tell him you're ready when he's ready to
ask again."

"What if he's not?"

Abby made a face. "Mare, we're talking about Shep. He's
probably struggling with not asking you every day."

I sighed. "This isn't about me. I'm here for you."

She frowned. "I almost forgot."

The doorknob jiggled, and the door burst open.

"Pidge?" Travis yelled. His expression crumbled when he saw
the food on the table, and then he looked over at us sitting on the
couch together.

Abby's eyes lit up as he rushed around the couch and knelt in front of her, wrapping his arms around her middle and burying his face in her lap.

Shepley stood in the doorway, smiling.

I beamed back at him. "You're sneaky."

"He chartered a flight back. I had to pick him up at the FPO here in town." He shut the door behind him and chuckled, crossing his arms. "I thought he was going to have a heart attack before we got here."

Abby's nose wrinkled. "The FPO? You mean that tiny airport just outside of town?" She looked to Travis. "A charter plane? How much did that cost?"

Travis looked up at her, shaking his head. "It doesn't matter. I just had to get here." He looked at me. "Thanks for sitting with her, Mare."

I nodded. "Of course." I stood, smiling at Shepley. "I'll follow you home."

Shepley opened the door. "After you, baby."

I waved good-bye to Travis and Abby, not that they noticed while he practically gnawed on her face.

Shepley held my hand as we walked down the stairs to our cars. The Charger was shining like new, parked next to my scratched and dingy red Honda. He unlocked the door, and the smell of smoke assaulted my nose.

I waved my hand in front of my face. "So gross. If you love your car so much, why do you let Travis smoke in it?"

He shrugged. "I don't know. He's never asked."

I smirked. "What would Travis do if, one day, you stopped letting him have his way all the time?"

Shepley kissed the corner of my mouth. "I don't know. What would you do?"

I blinked.

Shepley's expression turned to horror. "Oh, shit. That just came out. I didn't mean it the way it sounded."

I gripped my keys in my hand. "It's okay. I'll see you at home."

"Baby," he began.

But I was already halfway around the Honda.

I sat in the worn driver's seat of my dilapidated hatchback, starting it even though I wanted to sit there for a while and cry. Shepley backed out, and I followed him.

I wasn't sure what was worse—hearing the unintended truth or seeing the dread in his eyes after he'd said it. Shepley felt like a doormat to everyone he loved, including me.

Shepley

I pulled into the covered parking spot next to America's Honda and sighed. The steering wheel whined as my white knuckles twisted back and forth. The look on America's face before, when I'd spoken without thinking, wasn't like anything I'd ever seen before. If I said something stupid, anger would be evident in her eyes. But I hadn't made her angry. This was worse. Without meaning to, I'd hurt her, cutting her deep.

We lived three buildings over from Travis and Abby. Our building was less college students and more young couples and small families. The parking lot was full, the other tenants already home and in bed.

America stepped out. The car door creaked as she pushed it closed. She walked to the sidewalk, no emotion on her face. I had learned to stay calm during an argument, but America was emotional, and any effort to mask her feelings was never a good thing.

Growing up with my cousins had turned out to be a great resource for handling someone as tenacious as America, but falling in love with a woman who was self-confident and strong sometimes required battling my own insecurities and weaknesses.

She waited for me to climb out of the Charger, and then we walked to our downstairs apartment together. She was quiet, and that only made me more nervous.

"I didn't have time to do the dishes before I went over to Abby's," she said, walking into the kitchen. She rounded the breakfast bar and then froze.

"I did them before I went to pick up Travis."

She didn't turn around. "But I said I would do them."

Shit. "It's okay, baby. It didn't take long."

"Then I guess I should have had time to do them before I left."

Shit! "That's not what I meant. I didn't mind."

"I didn't either, which is why I said I would do them." She tossed her purse on the bar and disappeared down the hall.

I could hear her footsteps enter our room, and the bathroom door slammed.

I sat on the couch, covering my face with my hands. Our relationship hadn't been great for the past few months. I wasn't sure if it was because she wasn't happy with living with me or if she wasn't happy with *me*. Either way, it didn't bode well for our future. There was nothing that terrified me more.

"Shep?" a small voice from the hallway called.

I turned, watching America step out from the darkness into the dim living room.

"You're right. I'm overbearing, and I expect you to give me my way all the time. If you don't, I throw a tantrum. I can't keep doing this to you."

My blood ran cold. When she sat beside me, I instinctively leaned away, afraid of the pain she would cause when she said the words I feared most. "Mare, I love you. Whatever you're thinking, stop."

"I'm sorry," she began.

"Stop, damn it."

"I'm going to be better," she said, tears glistening in her eyes. "You don't deserve that."

"Wait. What?"

"You heard me," she said, seeming embarrassed.

She disappeared back into the hall, and I stood, following her. I opened the door to our dark bedroom. Just a sliver of light bled from the bathroom, revealing the made bed and the side tables weighed down by gossip magazines, textbooks, and black-and-white pictures of us. America peeled off her clothes, one piece at a time, leaving each one like a pathway to the shower, before turning it on.

I imagined her standing outside the curtain, reaching in, the soft curves of her body shifting slowly with each movement. The crotch of my jeans instantly resisted against the bulge behind the denim. I reached down and readjusted, walking toward the door bordered with harsh florescent light.

The door creaked as I pushed it open. America had already stepped behind the curtain, but I could hear the water sloughing off her with loud slaps on the floor of the tub.

"Mare?" I said. My dick was begging me to strip down and step into the shower behind her, but I knew she wouldn't be in the mood. "I didn't mean it. What I said earlier just came out. You're not a tyrant. You're stubborn, outspoken, and strong-willed, and I am in love with all those things. They're part of what makes you, *you*."

"It's different." Her voice barely carried through the curtain and over the sound of the whine of the water running through the pipes.

"What's different?" I asked, immediately pondering if it was the sex. Then I cursed the sixteen-year-old voice in my head that had spouted such infantile stupidity.

"You're different. We're different."

I sighed, letting my head fall forward. This was getting worse, not better. "Is that a bad thing?"

"It feels that way."

"How can I fix it?"

America peered at me from behind the curtain, only one beautiful emerald eye peeking out at me. Water raced down her forehead and nose, dripping off the end. "We moved in together."

I swallowed. "You're unhappy?"

She shook her head, but that only partially alleviated my anxiety. "You are."

"Mare," I breathed out. "No, I'm not. Nothing about being with you could ever make me unhappy."

Her eye instantly glossed over, and she closed it, pushing salty tears mixed with the tap water down her face. "I can see it. I can tell. I just don't know why."

I pulled the curtain to the side, and she stepped back as far as she could, watching me step one foot inside and then the other, even though I was still fully dressed.

"What are you doing?" she asked.

I wrapped my arms around her, feeling the water pour over the top of my head, soaking my shirt.

"Wherever you are, I'm there with you. I don't want to be anywhere you're not."

I kissed her, and she whimpered in my arms. It wasn't like her to show her softer side. Normally, if she were hurt or sad, she would get angry.

"I don't know why it's been different, but I love you the same. Actually, more."

"Then why ..." She trailed off, losing her nerve.

"Why what?"

She shook her head. "I'm sorry about the dishes."

"Baby," I said, putting my finger beneath her chin and lifting gently until she looked up at me. "Fuck the dishes."

America lifted my shirt, up and over my head, letting it fall to the floor with a slap. Then, she unbuckled my belt while her tongue flicked along my neck. She was already naked, so there was nothing for me to do but let her undress me. That was strangely arousing.

As soon as my zipper was down, America knelt in front of me, taking my jeans with her. I kicked off my tennis shoes, and she tossed them outside the tub before doing the same with my jeans. She reached up, curving her fingers until they were snuggly between my skin and the waistband of my boxers, and she slid them down, carefully pulling them over my erection. Once they slapped against the tile outside the curtain, America pulled my entire length into her mouth, and I had to steady myself, palms flat against the wall.

I groaned as the tugging suction and her grip worked together to create quite possibly the best sensation in the world. Her eager mouth was so warm and wet. Hers was the only one that made me wish I could kiss it and fuck it at the same time. For a fleeting moment, the thought that she had gone down on me to change the subject popped into my head, but it was hard to argue with her if that were the case. Sex with her was one of my most favorite subjects.

Her free hand reached up to cup my balls, and that nearly threw me over the edge.

"I need to be inside you," I said.

She didn't respond, so I lifted her to a standing position and then hitched her knee to my hip.

She grabbed my ears and pulled me against her mouth, and I positioned myself, deciding in the moment to lower her onto my dick—slowly since she'd already worked me into a frenzy. I lifted her other leg. Just as I moved to position myself, I lost my footing. America squealed as I reached out, scrambling for something to save us, and then I resorted to bracing for the fall. The nylon curtain ripped from the rings, only giving us half a second before my back slammed onto the floor.

I grunted and then looked up at America, her hair dripping wet, her eyes clenched shut. One jade eye popped open and then the other.

"Christ, are you okay?" I asked.

"Are you?"

I breathed out a laugh. "Yeah, I think so."

She covered her mouth and then began to giggle, making laughter erupt from my throat and rip through the apartment. Soon, we were wiping our eyes and trying to catch our breaths.

The giggles faded, and we were left on the floor, water dripping from our skin onto the tile. A droplet formed on America's nose and dripped to my cheek. She wiped it away, her eyes shifting back and forth, waiting, as she wondered what I might say next.

"We're okay," I said softly. "I promise."

America sat up, and I did the same.

"We don't have to do what everyone else is doing to be happy, right?" Her voice was tinged with sadness.

I swallowed down the lump forming in my throat. It wasn't that I wanted to do what everyone else was doing. For a long time, I'd wanted what they already had.

"No," I said. For the first time since we'd met, I lied to America.

I was too ashamed to admit to her that I wanted those things—the rings, the vows, the mortgage, and the kids. I wanted it all. But it was too hard to tell an unconventional girl that I wanted a conventional life with her. The thought that we didn't want the same things and what that meant terrified me, so I pushed it to the back of my mind, to the same place where I kept my memories of Mom crying over Aunt Diane, far enough down so that my heart wouldn't feel it.

CHAPTER FOUR

America

My toes sparkled in the sun, freshly painted with Pretty in Pink. They wiggled as I relished the thin sheen of sweat on my skin and the heat dancing off the pavement surrounding the turquoise water. I was surely burning under the bright rays, but I remained on the white plastic slats of my lounge chair, happy to soak in the vitamin D, even with the little shits in 404B splashing like heathens.

My sunglasses fell down for the tenth time, the salty beads on the bridge of my nose making them slide around like a stick of melting butter.

Abby held up her water bottle. "Here's to having the same day off."

I held up mine and touched it to hers. "I'll drink to that."

We both tipped up our beverages, and I felt the cool liquid glide down my throat. I set the bottle down next to me, but it slipped from my hand and rolled under my chair.

"Damn it," I said, protesting but not moving. It was too hot to move. It was too hot to do anything but stay in the air-conditioning or lie by the pool, intermittently slithering in the water before we spontaneously combusted.

"What time does Travis get off work?" I asked.

"Five," she breathed.

"When does he go out of town again?"

"Not for two weeks, unless something comes up."

"You're awfully patient about this."

"About what? Him making a living? It is what it is," she said.

I turned onto my stomach and faced her, my cheek flat against the slats. "You're not worried?"

Abby lowered her glasses and peered over them at me. "Should I be?"

"Nothing. I'm stupid. Ignore me."

"I think the sun is frying your brain," Abby said, pushing up her glasses. She settled back against her lounger, her body relaxed.

"I told him."

I didn't look at her, but I could feel Abby staring at the side of my face.

"Told who what?" she asked.

"Shep. I told him—sort of, in a way—that I was ready."

"Why don't you tell him for sure, directly, that you're ready?"

I sighed. "I might as well ask him myself."

"You two are exhausting."

"Has he said anything to Travis?"

"No. And you know anything Trav tells me in confidence is off-limits."

"That's not fair. I would tell you, if I knew it was important. You're a shit friend."

"But I'm a great wife," she said, not an ounce of apology in her voice.

"I told him we should visit my parents before classes start. A road trip."

"Fun."

"I'm hoping he gets the hint to pop the question."

"Shall I plant a seed?"

"It's already been planted, Abby. If he doesn't ask me, it's because he doesn't want to ... anymore."

"Of course he does. You've been together three years in August. That's not quite three months away, and it's definitely not the longest a girl has waited for a ring. I think it just feels like it because Trav and I eloped so fast."

"Maybe."

"Be patient. Rejection is hard for their egos to take."

"Travis didn't seem to mind."

She ignored my jab. "Twice takes twice as long."

"Rub it in, bitch," I snapped.

"I didn't mean—" Abby squealed as she was lifted off the lounger and into Travis's arms.

He took two long strides and leaped into the pool. She was still screaming when they rose to the surface.

I stood and walked to the edge, crossing my arms. "You're off early."

"Had a cancellation at the gym."

"Hi, baby," Shepley said, wrapping his arms around me.

Unlike Travis, he was fully dressed, so I was safe.

"Hi," I began.

But Shepley leaned, and soon, we were falling into the pool like a toppling pillar.

"Shepley!" I shrieked as we hit the surface of the water before going under.

He popped up and pulled me with him, cradling me in his arms. He shook his head and smiled.

"You're nuts!" I said.

"It wasn't planned, but it's over a hundred fucking degrees outside. I'm baking," Shepley said.

The little shits from the next building over splashed us once, but after just one frown from Travis, they were scrambling to get out of the pool.

I planted a kiss on Shepley's lips, tasting the chlorine on his mouth. "Have you thought about the road trip?" I asked.

He shook his head. "I checked the weather. They're supposed to have some gnarly stuff coming in."

I frowned. "Really? I grew up in Tornado Alley. You think I give two shits about the weather?"

"What if it hails? The Charger ..."

"Okay, we'll take the Honda."

"To Wichita?" His nose wrinkled.

"She can make it! She's made it before!" I said, defensive.

Shepley dragged his legs through the water to the side, and then he lifted me to the concrete. He wiped water from his face and squinted up at me. "You want to drive the Honda to your parents', this weekend, with storms coming. What's so urgent?"

"Nothing. I just thought it would be nice to get away."

"Just the two of you. A *special* road trip," Abby said.

When Shepley turned to look at her, I shot my best friend a warning glare. Her stoic expression didn't give anything away, but I still wanted to dunk her.

He traded glances with Travis and then turned back to face me, confusion scrolling across his face. "It'll give us time to talk, I guess. We've been busy. That'll be nice."

"Exactly," I said.

Once I spoke those words, something lit in Shepley's eyes, and a million thoughts seemed to flip behind his eyes.

Whatever was bothering him, he shook it off and pushed himself up, pecking my lips. "If that's what you want, I'll ask off."

"It's what I want."

He climbed out of the pool, his white T-shirt translucent, his jeans sopping wet, his sneakers squishing with each step. "I'll go in and make the call. But we'll take the Charger. It might be twenty-five years older, but it's more dependable."

"Thanks, baby," I said, smiling, as he walked away. Once he was out of earshot, I turned to Abby, all emotion gone from my face. "You're an asshole."

Abby cackled.

Travis looked from Abby to me and back again. "What? What's so funny?"

Abby shook her head. "I'll tell you later."

"No, you won't!" I said, kicking water at her.

With his hand, Travis squeegeed droplets of water off his face, and then he kissed Abby's temple. She left him, swimming to the side of the pool and climbing up the ladder. She took her towel off the lounger and dried off. Travis watched her like it was the first time he'd ever set eyes on her.

"I'm surprised you're not pregnant yet," I said.

Abby froze.

Travis frowned. "C'mon, Mare! Don't say the P word. You'll freak her out!"

"Why? Has it been on the table?" I asked my friend.

"A few times," Abby said, looking pointedly at Travis. "He thinks I'm going to stop my birth control the moment we graduate."

My eyebrows pushed up. "Are you?"

"No," she said quickly. "Not until we buy a house."

Travis's expression intensified. "We have an extra bedroom."

"Thanks, Mare," Abby grumbled, bending over to rub the towel over her legs.

"Sorry," I said. "I'm going in. We have a road trip to plan."

"Hey. If you go, be careful. Shep's right. The weather is supposed to be bad. Maybe you should wait until the storm season is over."

"If we don't go now, we'll get busy. Once classes start, it will be too late. We'll have to wait until a break." I looked to the ground. "The way he's been acting, I don't know if he'll be patient much longer."

"He'll wait forever, Mare," Abby said.

"Too late for what?" Travis asked, climbing out of the pool. "What's he waiting on?"

"Nothing." I shot Abby a warning glare before gathering my things and pushing out of the gate. I closed it behind me, keeping my hand on the hot metal. "Keep your mouth shut. You might be his wife, but you were my friend first."

"Okay, okay," Abby said, cowering under my stare.

Shepley

"Thanks, Janice. I appreciate it." I tapped the red button and set the phone on the bed.

Janice had loved me since the moment I stepped into her office for the interview. What had started out as a gopher job had turned into administrative work, and then I'd somehow ended up in the wealth management department. Janice was hoping I'd stay on after I graduated college, promising me promotions and opportunities galore, but my heart wasn't in it.

I stared at the almost empty drawer of my nightstand. *That's where my heart is.*

Once the display light on my cell phone disappeared, the darkness of the room surrounded me. The summer evening sun snuck in through the sides of the curtains, creating faint shadows on the walls.

We'd lived here for less than a year, and already, the walls were crowded with frames holding our memories. It hadn't been hard to mesh our belongings because the last two years had been *us* and *our* and *we*. Now, I wasn't sure if it was a symbol of our lives together or if it was a memorial of the couple we used to be.

I'd regretted proposing since the moment America said no. We had become different after that.

I rubbed the muscle between my shoulder and neck. It was thick with tension. I'd already peeled off my wet clothes and wrapped a towel around my waist. It was fluffy, something I hadn't required before living with my girlfriend, but I had come to appreciate it along with the smell of her lotion on the sheets and the boxes of tissue in every room of the apartment. Even the clutter on her nightstand had become comforting.

I became glaringly aware of the drawer in the nightstand. It held only one item—a small dark red box. Inside was the ring I fantasized putting on her finger, the ring she'd wear on our wedding day, fitting perfectly over a matching band. I'd purchased it two years before and taken it out as many times.

We had a long road trip ahead, and I was going to take it along for the ride. Our drive to Kansas would mark the third time the box would be seeing the outside of that drawer, and I wondered if it would return to its home. I wasn't sure what it might mean if it did, but I couldn't keep wondering and waiting.

My hands felt scratchy and dry when I interlaced my fingers and looked at the floor, wondering if I should produce a flowery proposal like last time or if I should just go for it. Asking her to marry me this time would amount to so much more. If she said no, she would have to talk about what was next. I knew America wanted to get married someday because she'd talked about it to me and to Abby with me in the room.

Maybe she just doesn't want to marry me.

Worrying that it would never be the right time for America to say yes had become a daily torment. *No* was such a tiny word, yet it had affected me. It had affected us. But I loved her too much to push the subject. I was too afraid she would say something I didn't want to hear.

Then there were the tiny scraps of hope—like her talking about the future and the larger confirmations, like moving in together. But even as we'd unpacked the boxes, I'd wondered if she had just agreed to get an apartment because she was too stubborn to admit to her parents that they were right about us not being ready.

Still, the fear of the truth kept me from asking. I loved her too much to let her go that easily. She would have to fight to leave as much as I would fight to keep her. I questioned my sanity for even considering proposing a third time, and I feared it would be the first agonizing day of many where I would have to learn to live without her.

If she said yes though, it would make pushing through all that fear to ask worth it.

"Baby?" America called. The front door closed behind her words.

"In the bedroom," I replied.

She opened the door and flipped on the light. "Why are you sitting in the dark?"

"Just got off the phone with Janice. She wasn't super happy about the late notice, but she gave me Friday off."

"Sweet!" she said, dropping her towel. "I'm going to take a shower. Want to join me? Or are you going to the gym?"

"I can go in the morning," I said, scrambling to my feet.

America tugged on a string as she walked, and her bikini top fell to the ground. She paused a few steps later to shimmy the bottoms down her thighs, and then she let them fall the rest of the way.

I followed behind her, picking up pieces of clothing as I went. She reached beyond the curtain to turn the knob and frowned at me while I tossed her clothes into the hamper.

"Really? You're cleaning up after me?"

I shrugged. "It's just a habit, Mare. It's compulsive. I can't help myself."

"How did you live with Travis?" she asked.

Thinking about Travis immediately made the beginnings of a hard-on disappear. "It was a lot of work."

"Is living with me a lot of work?"

"You're not that bad. It's preferable. Trust me."

She pulled back the curtain and then pinched my towel, pulling until the tucked portion was free. The fluffy cotton was on the ground, and then so was America.

With one hand, I gripped the edge of the Formica surrounding the sink, and with the other, I gently buried my fingers in her still wet hair. Her mouth was remarkable. She used one hand to grip my girth, and with just enough suction and a hint of teeth, she teased and sucked me until I began to worry that I was going to lift the Formica right off the cabinet.

Soon, I was coming, but she didn't relent, her mouth working me until I was finished. I lifted her to stand and then ripped at the curtain, pushing her backward and then turning her around. With one hand between her legs and the other clutching the slick skin of her hip, I kissed her shoulder while I sank myself deep inside her. The sound she made was enough to make me come a second time, but I waited for her.

I worked my fingers in a circle on her soft skin, smiling when she began writhing against my hand, whispering for more. While I rocked against her, agonizingly slow, she continued whimpering and moaning.

The water cascaded over her back, pushing her hair to one side or another, and I ran my palm over her bronze skin, savoring every inch, hoping she would remember how good we were together when the time came to make a decision.

The pitch of her cries became higher, that adorable yelping she made when she climaxed. Unable to stop, I rammed myself into her, over and over, until I came again, slowing as she did, panting even though we'd been at it for no more than twenty minutes.

America turned around to look at me, wearing nothing but a flirtatious grin. She stood, pulling away from me—which was the worst feeling in the world—and then she wrapped her arms around my neck as the water poured over our heads.

"I love you," she whispered.

I raked my hands through each side of her hair, sliding my tongue into her mouth. I hoped it was enough.

CHAPTER FIVE

America

SHEPLEY HEAVED THE LAST OF MY LUGGAGE into the backseat of the Charger, puffing as he fought to make it fit. Once he accomplished that feat, he grabbed his backpack from the concrete and tossed it behind his seat. I kissed his cheek, and he nodded, lifting the inside collar of his T-shirt to wipe the sweat from his forehead. It wasn't even dawn yet, and it was already hot.

Abby crossed her arms. "All set?"

"That's all of it," I said.

"Thank God," Shepley said.

"Pussy," Travis teased, punching his cousin in his side.

Shepley jerked in reaction and then playfully punched him back. "Just because I haven't punched you in a couple of years doesn't mean it won't happen again."

"A couple of years? When did you punch him?" I asked.

Travis touched his jaw. "It's been a little longer than that. The night you broke up with him. The night"—he looked at Abby, already regretting what he was about to say—"I brought Megan back to the apartment."

I looked at Shepley, dubious. "You punched Travis."

"Right after you left," Shepley admitted. "I thought you knew?"

I shook my head and then looked at Travis. "Did it hurt?"

"Sometimes, I think I can still feel it," Travis said. "Shepley hits hard."

"Good," I said, feeling a little turned on at the thought of Shepley throwing a punch. My Maddox wasn't known for fighting like the brothers, but it was nice to know he could hold his own when needed.

Shepley looked at his watch. "We'd better head out. I want to beat that storm coming in. Wichita is supposed to be under a tornado watch all afternoon."

"You're sure you can't wait?" Abby asked.

I shrugged. "Shepley's already taken the day off."

"I'm glad you're taking the Charger," Travis said. "The only thing worse than driving in the rain is being stranded in the rain."

Shepley kissed my temple and then opened the driver's door. "Let's get on the road, baby."

I hugged Abby. "I'll call you when we get there. Should be mid afternoon. Two thirty or three."

"Have a safe trip," she said, hugging me tight.

As I buckled my seat belt and Shepley backed out of the parking space, Travis pretended to kick Shepley's door. "Bye, dickhead."

"I love how guys show affection. It's so cute in a sad sort of way."

"You think I can't show affection?"

I arched an eyebrow.

Shepley threw the car into park, jumped out, and ran to Travis, leaping on his cousin and wrapping both arms and legs around him. Travis was unfazed, holding him like an overgrown toddler.

Shepley hugged Travis, kissed him—on the mouth—and then released him before walking to the Charger with his arms outstretched to each side. "Now what? I'm man enough to show affection!"

"You win," I said, half-amazed, half-amused.

Travis couldn't sustain his stoic expression, looking both disgusted and confused. He wiped off his mouth and then reached for Abby, hugging her to his side. "You're weird as fuck, dude."

Shepley slid back into his seat, closed the door, and fastened his seat belt with a click. He rolled down the window, saying good-bye with a quick salute. "You kissed me first, asshole. I have a picture to prove it."

"We were three."

"See you on Sunday!" Shepley said.

"Bye, fucker!" Travis yelled.

Shepley pulled the gear into drive and navigated his way out of the parking lot.

Within ten minutes, we were already almost out of town, passing Skin Deep Tattoo on the way. Shepley honked his horn, seeing both Trenton's and Camille's vehicles parked in front.

"They used to always be smoking outside every time I drove by," Shepley said.

"Cami said they quit for Olive."

"So did Taylor," Shepley said.

"Isn't that *nuts*?" I screeched, shaking my head as I thought about Taylor and how he'd happened to fall in love with Olive's mother a thousand miles away. "Now, we just need to work on Travis."

"He said he'll quit when Abby's pregnant."

"Now, that would be a miracle," I said.

"Which one? Him quitting or her finally agreeing to kids?"

"Both."

"Do you want kids?" Shepley didn't look at me when he asked.

I swallowed. We weren't even out of town yet, and he was already hitting the hard topics. I wasn't sure if it was a trick question. Was he looking for a reason to leave? Would my answer be the last straw for him?

"Um ... yeah. I mean, I guess. I've always thought I would ... have kids. Later."

He only nodded, which made me more nervous. I pulled out a magazine and absently flipped through it, pretending to read the words on the pages. Truthfully, I didn't have a clue who or what was in it. I was just desperate to look casual. We had talked about kids before, and the fact that it was so uncomfortable now seemed to be an ominous sign that we were going in the wrong direction.

By the time we hit Springfield, the storms were already beginning to organize.

Shepley pointed out dark skies on the horizon. "The hotter it gets, the more those storms will build. Look at the weather forecast for Kansas City."

I pulled my phone from my purse, tapping in the information. I shook my head. "It says storms, but they won't start until later." I selected my favorite radar app. "Oh. There are some angry-looking red blobs in southwestern Oklahoma right now. It's going to hit Wichita around the time we pull into town."

"That's what I was afraid of. Hopefully, it won't hit before."

"We can always pull over and get a motel room," I said.

My smile felt unnatural on my face, the air in the car thick and uncomfortable. I suddenly grew angry that I felt that way. Shepley was my boyfriend. I loved him, and he loved me. That, I was sure of. We were neck-high in a stupid misunderstanding, and I didn't want to be that girl. I opened my mouth to say as much, but the expression on Shepley's face stopped me.

"I love you," was the only thing I could manage to say.

His foot slipped off the gas pedal for a moment, and then he reached for my hand, keeping his eyes on the road. "I love you, too."

By the subtle twitch of his eye, I knew he was working to keep the wounded look off his face.

"Hey, look. The writing on the door of that semi says O'Fallon, Missouri," he said. "Like Taylor's Falyn."

"I think she spells her name differently."

"Yeah …" He trailed off, unable to pretend any longer.

I flipped through my magazine a second time, pretending to read and intermittently staring out my window at the trees and wheat fields lining Route Thirty-Six. Shepley kept his hand in mine, squeezing every once in a while. I prayed that it wasn't because he was weighing missing me against putting up with my shit.

When we passed Chillicothe, Missouri, I noticed an exit sign for Trenton. "Huh. Look at that. Should we play a game? Find all the members of the Maddox family? I think there's a town called Cameron, north of Kansas City. I say that counts as Cami."

"Sure. Can we count your name already?"

"Ha-ha," I said.

Even though we were both desperate to lighten the mood, it was still awkward. I wasn't part of the Maddox family yet, not really. It was possible I'd lost my chance.

When we reached the Kansas City bypass, the sky opened, filling the car with smells of rain, wet asphalt, and the sharp stench of turmoil. I'd hoped the hours in the car would force communication, talking about what we couldn't say, but there I sat. The girl who took pride in her big mouth was too afraid to bring up anything uncomfortable.

Keep your mouth shut, Mare. He'll never get over it if you prompt a proposal even if he wants to do it.

Maybe he doesn't want to do it … anymore.

The constant *rat-tat-tatting* of rain on the Charger grew irritating. As we drove between storms, the windshield wipers would change from dragging along dry glass to furiously trying to keep up with the downpour. Shepley would offer small talk—about the rain, of course, and the upcoming school year—but he stuck to safe topics, careful not to skirt too close to the edge of anything serious.

"Topeka," Shepley announced as if the sign weren't right there in big, bold white letters.

"We've made good time. Let's stop at a restaurant. I'm tired of gas station food."

"Okay," he agreed. "Check your phone for something on the route."

"Gator's Bar and Grill," I said aloud. It was third down on the list, but it was rated only two-and-a-half stars. "One review says not to go there after dark. That's interesting. You think there are vampires?"

Shepley chuckled, looking down at the clock above the radio. "It's just after noon. I think we'll be safe."

"It's three-point-two miles ahead," I said. "Just off the turnpike."

"Which one? Four Seventy turns into Interstate Thirty-Five."

"Four Seventy."

Shepley nodded, satisfied. "Gator's it is."

As promised, Gator's was just off the turnpike, just over three miles away. Shepley picked a parking space and turned off the engine for the first time in almost four hours. I stepped onto the concrete parking lot, my bones and muscles feeling stiff.

Shepley stretched on his side of the car, bending down and then standing up, pulling his arms across his chest. "Sitting for that long can't be good. I don't know how people with a desk job do it."

"You have a desk job," I said with a smirk.

"Part-time. If it were forty or fifty hours a week, I'd go nuts."

"So, you're not going to stay at the bank?" I asked, surprised. "I thought you liked it there."

"Wealth management is a good place to be, but you know I'm not going to stay there."

"No. You haven't mentioned it."

"Yeah, I did. I … oh. That was Cami."

"Cami?"

"The last time I went with Trenton to The Red. You know how much I talk when I'm drunk."

"I've forgotten," I said.

Shepley reached for my hand as we walked inside, but at least two feet of space and unspoken thoughts were between us.

I glanced around Gator's, looking up at the tall ceiling. Multicolored Christmas lights hung from the exposed ventilation system, the booth seats had ratty holes torn in the upholstery, and the floor had at least ten years of grime soaked into every twisted tuft of the worn carpet. Stale grease invaded my senses, and the rusted tin wainscot and charcoal-gray paint were more unwelcoming than the intended industrial chic.

"The two-star rating is making sense," I said, shivering from the air-conditioning.

We waited so long for a table that I almost asked Shepley if we could leave, but then a blue-haired waitress with a chip on her shoulder and more piercings than she had holes showed us to two empty seats at the bar.

"Why did she seat us here?" I asked. "There are empty tables. There are a lot of empty tables."

"Not even the employees want to be here," Shepley said.

"Maybe we should just go?"

He shook his head. "We'll just grab a quick bite and get back on the road."

I nodded, unsettled.

The bartender wiped off the spaces in front of us and asked for our drink order. Shepley asked for a bottled water, and I ordered a strawberry lemonade.

"Not a beer? Why did you sit at the bar then?" the bartender asked, perturbed.

"We were seated here. It wasn't a request," I snapped.

Shepley patted my knee. "I'm driving. You can pour her a Bud Light. Draft, please."

The bartender placed menus in front of us and walked away.

"Why did you order a beer?"

"I don't want him telling the cooks to spit in our food, Mare. You don't have to drink it."

Thunder cracked outside and shook the building, and then rain began to pelt the roof.

"We can wait for the storm to pass somewhere, but I don't want it to be here," I said.

"Okay. We'll find somewhere else even if it's the parking lot." He patted my knee again and then squeezed.

"Hey," a man said, passing behind us with a friend. He looked drunk already, shuffling to a seat at the end of the bar. His eyes poured over me like dirty water.

"Hey," Shepley answered for me. He locked eyes with the drunk.

"Baby," I said in warning.

"Just showing him I'm not intimidated," Shepley said. "Hopefully, he'll be less inclined to bother us."

The bartender returned with my strawberry lemonade and Shepley's bottled water. "You ready to order?"

"Yeah, we'll both have the southwest chicken wrap."

"Fries or onion rings?"

"Neither."

The bartender took our menus, eyed us, and then left to put in the order.

"Where the fuck is he going?" the drunk said to his friend.

"Calm down, Rich. He'll be back," he said, chuckling.

I tried to ignore them. "So, you're considering the sports scout route?"

Shepley shrugged. "It's a dream job. I'm not sure how realistic a venture it is, but yes, that's the plan. Coach Greer said I should apply for a graduate assistant coaching position. He said I'd have a good chance. I'll start there."

"But ... you don't play football."

Shepley shifted in his seat. "I did."

"You ... did? When?"

"Never college. I started all four years of high school. Believe it or not, I was pretty good."

"What happened? And why haven't you told me this before?"

Shepley pushed out his water as he leaned further up on the bar. "It's stupid, I guess. It was the one thing I was better at than all my cousins."

"But Travis doesn't talk about it. Your parents don't talk about it. If you started as a freshman, you must have been better than good. I haven't even seen any pictures at your house that might insinuate you were in sports."

"I blew three of four major ligaments in my knee during the last game before the play-offs my senior year. I worked hard to come back, but when I began training for Eastern, the knee didn't feel the same. It still hadn't healed, so I was a redshirt freshman. I wasn't sure how long the coaches would wait, but I knew that even if they gave me the year, I would be done." He sat up straight. "So, I bowed out."

"That explains why you always say a different reason for the scars. I thought you were just embarrassed."

"I was."

I frowned. "That's nothing to be embarrassed about. I can see why you want to be a part of it again."

He nodded, the smile on his face revealing that he was just now realizing that fact himself.

He had opened up. It was the perfect opportunity for me to start a conversation about why the air had been so tense in the car, but as soon as I opened my mouth, I chickened out. "Thanks for telling me."

"I should have told you a long time ago, but …" He trailed off.

Finally, curiosity and impatience won over fear. "Why does it feel so weird between us?" I asked. "What's on your mind?"

Shepley tensed even more than he already had been. "What? Nothing. Why do you ask?"

"You're not thinking of anything?"

"What are *you* thinking?"

"Baby," I said, my tone more chastising than I'd meant.

Shepley sighed, nodding when the bartender brought me a cold mug full of amber liquid and a thin line of froth.

"Chug it!" Rich said, grunting. "God, those lips are fucking fantastic. I bet she could suck a golf ball through a garden hose! Lick them after you take a drink, sexy. Do all men everywhere a favor."

I merely snarled at him, pushing the mug farther away from me.

Rich stood up.

The friend tried to stop him. "For fuck's sake! Sit down!"

Rich shook his head and wiped his mouth with his forearm, stumbling toward us.

"Shit," I said under my breath. I kept my eyes forward.

Shepley squeezed my knee. "It's okay. Don't worry."

"You can take those lips an—" Rich began.

"Sit. The Fuck. Down," Shepley warned.

I'd only heard him talk so severely to Travis. My breath caught, and a mixture of nerves, surprise, and the distinct feeling of being turned on heated the blood in my cheeks.

"What did you say, motherfucker?" Rich asked, leaning against the bar on the other side of me.

Shepley bristled. "You have three seconds to get away from my girlfriend, or I'm going to knock you the fuck out."

"Rich!" his friend called. "Get over here!"

Rich leaned in, and Shepley stood, taking a step around my stool, glowering straight into Rich's eyes.

"Move out of the way, Mare."

"Shepley …"

Rich snorted. "Mare? Shepley? Are you celebrity kids? What kind of fucking names are those?"

"Walk away," Shepley said.

I stepped down off my stool and took a few steps back.

"This is your last warning," Shepley added.

The bartender stood frozen in the kitchen doorway, holding our plates in his hands.

"Shep," I said, reaching for his arm. I'd never seen him so hostile. "Let's just go."

With two of his fingers, Rich tapped Shepley's shoulder. "What are you going to do, little man? How about I shove my dick in her mouth, and then you'll have something to be angry about?"

Shepley's jaw worked under the skin.

"Baby," I said.

His shoulders relaxed. He pulled out a few bills from his pocket and tossed them onto the bar. He outstretched his arm behind him, reaching for me.

I sidestepped toward the door, encouraging my boyfriend to follow. Shepley began to turn toward me, but Rich reached out, grabbing a fistful of Shepley's shirt and yanking him back.

Shepley didn't hesitate. Rich's eyes grew wide as he saw Shepley coming at him with a raised elbow. A thud sounded when Shepley's elbow knocked against Rich's cheekbone. Rich stumbled back, holding the side of his face, and the friend stood, pausing.

"I fucking dare you to jump in," Shepley growled.

Rich tried to take advantage of Shepley's momentary distraction and swung. Shepley dodged, and Rich fell forward as he followed through with the motion. I covered my mouth as I was in total disbelief that it was my boyfriend, not Travis, in the middle of a fight. It had been a long time since I saw Travis in the ring of The Circle, and even though he'd calmed down quite a bit since the wedding, Travis would still end up throwing a punch or two if someone pushed him too far.

Shepley was always the peacekeeper, but at the moment, he was landing punches on Rich, hard enough to draw blood. A cut began to bleed just above his right eye.

The bartender reached for the phone right when Shepley reared back his fist and grunted while he swung. Rich spun, doing a one-eighty, and then fell on the floor, bouncing once. He was out cold. The friend watched him from the stool, shaking his head. Rich's eyes were already beginning to swell shut as he lay there, dazed, on the dirty carpet.

"Baby, let's go," I said.

Shepley took a step toward the friend, who jerked back in reaction.

"Shepley Maddox! We're leaving!"

Shepley looked back at me, huffing. He didn't have a single mark on his face. He walked past me, taking my hand and pulling me out the door.

CHAPTER SIX

Shepley

THE CHARGER'S STEERING WHEEL WHINED as I twisted the wood with both hands. Rain fell from a dark blue sky, assaulting the windshield so loudly that America had to nearly yell over the noise. She was chattering a thousand words a minute, and it was all blurring together. She wasn't mad but excited. I wasn't mad. I was feeling unadulterated deep fucking fury. Adrenaline was still pumping through my veins, making my head throb like it was going to explode. That feeling was exactly why I wouldn't lose my temper. It would leave me feeling sick, out of control, guilty—everything I didn't want to be.

As the miles passed and we escaped Topeka, America's voice came into focus.

She reached over to touch my hand. "Baby? Did you hear me? You might want to slow down. The rain is coming down so hard it's starting to stand on the roads."

She wasn't afraid, but I could hear the concern in her voice. My foot lifted half an inch off the gas pedal, and I eased up, releasing the tension from my leg and then the rest of my body.

"Sorry," I said through my teeth.

America squeezed my hand. "What happened?"

I shrugged. "I lost it."

"I feel like I'm riding in the car with Travis instead of my boyfriend."

I breathed out through my nose. "It won't happen again."

From the corner of my eye, I saw her face compress.

"Do you still love me?"

Her words were like a punch to the gut, and I coughed once, trying to catch my breath. "What?"

Her eyes glossed over. "Do you still love me? Is it because I said no?"

"You ... you want to talk about this now? I mean ... of course I love you. You know that, Mare. I can't believe you just asked me that."

She wiped an escaped tear from her cheek and looked out the window. The weather outside mirrored the storm in her eyes. "I don't know what happened."

My throat tightened, choking off any reply I might have had. Words didn't come to me. I alternated between staring at her in confusion and watching the road.

"I love you." She balled her elegant thin fingers into a fist and propped them under her chin, her elbow on the door's armrest. "I've wanted to talk to you about the way things have been between us lately, but I was scared ... and ... I didn't know what to say. And—"

"America? Is this a ... is this like a good-bye trip?"

She turned to me. "You tell me."

I didn't realize my teeth had been clenched until my jaw began to hurt. I tightly closed my eyes and then blinked a few times, trying to concentrate on the road, keeping the Charger between the white and yellow lines. I wanted to pull over to talk, but with the hard rain and limited sight distance, I knew it would be too dangerous. I wouldn't take the chance with the love of my life in the car—even if she didn't believe she was at the moment.

"We don't talk," she said. "When did we stop talking?"

"When we started loving each other so much that it was too scary to chance it? At least, that's what it was for me—or is," I said.

Saying the truth out loud was both terrifying and a relief. I'd been keeping it in for so long that letting it go made me feel a little lighter, but not knowing how she would react made me wish I could take it back.

But this was what she wanted—to talk, the truth—and she was right. It was time. The silence had been ruining us. Instead of enjoying our new chapter together, I had been lingering in the *why not*, the *not yet*, and the *when*. I had been impatient, and it was poisoning me. Did I love the thought of us more than I loved her? That didn't even make sense.

"Jesus, I'm sorry, Mare," I spit out.

She hesitated. "For what?"

My face screwed into disgust. "For the way I've been acting. For keeping things from you. For being impatient."

"What have you been keeping from me?"

She looked so nervous. It broke my heart.

I pulled her hand to my lips and kissed her knuckles. She turned to face me, pulling up one leg and holding her knee to her chest. She needed something else to hold on to, bracing herself for my answer. The rain-speckled windows were beginning to fog, softening her. She was the most beautiful and saddest thing I'd ever seen. She was strong and confident, and I'd reduced her to the worried big-eyed girl next to me.

"I love you, and I want to be with you forever."

"But?" she prompted.

"No buts. That's it."

"You're lying," she said.

"From now on, that's it. I promise."

She sighed and faced forward. Her lip began to tremble. "I screwed up, Shep. Now, you're just content to keep going like we have been."

"Yes. I mean … is that okay? Isn't that what you want? What do you mean, you screwed up?"

Her lips pressed together into a hard line. "I shouldn't have said no," she whimpered softly.

I exhaled, trailing off in thought. "To me? When I asked you to marry me?"

"Yes," she said, her voice almost pleading. "I wasn't ready then."

"I know. It's okay," I said, squeezing her hand. "I'm not giving up on us."

"How do we fix this? I'm willing to do whatever. I just want it to be the way it used to be. Well, not exactly, but …"

I smiled, watching her stumble over the words. She was trying to tell me something without saying it, and that was something she wasn't comfortable with. America always said what she wanted. It was one of the million reasons I loved her.

"I wish I could go back to that moment. I need a do-over."

"A do-over?" I asked.

She was both hopeful and frustrated. I opened my mouth to ask why, but quarter-sized hail began to pelt the windshield.

"Shit. *Shit!*" I yelled, imagining every dent being pounded into the body. I slowed down, looking for an exit.

"What do we do?" America asked, sitting up and planting her hands on the seat.

"How far out are we?" I asked.

America scrambled for her phone. She tapped on it a few times. "We're just outside Emporia. So, a little over an hour?" she yelled over the sound of rain and a thousand ice chunks nailing the paint at forty miles per hour.

I slowed down even more, seeing the glow of brake lights from vehicles pulled over on the shoulder. The windshield wipers were echoing my heartbeat in a fast but steady rhythm, like the dance music at The Red.

"Shepley?" America said. Worry tinged her voice like before, but she was also afraid.

"We're going to be okay. It'll pass soon," I said, hoping I was right.

"But your car!"

The tail end of the Charger slipped, and I tore my hand away from America's, using both of mine to navigate the wheel against the skid. We slid across the road, toward the median. I overcorrected, and then the Charger began to fishtail toward the ditch. Hand over hand, I turned the wheel again, taking my foot off the gas. The Charger tilted to the side, and we slipped down a short embankment before landing in a full drainage ditch.

The water crested at the bottom of my window, the grassy brown river arching and ebbing against the glass, begging to be let in.

"You okay?" I asked, holding her face in my hands, checking her over.

America's eyes bulged. "What ... do we—"

Her phone began to shriek. She took one glance and then showed me the screen.

"Tornado warning," she said. "For Emporia. Right now."

"We have to get out of here," I said.

She nodded and turned around in her seat.

"Leave the luggage. We can come back for it. We have to go. Now."

I rolled down my window. America took the cue, unbuckled her seat belt, and rolled down hers as well. As she began to climb out, I unbuckled but paused. The ring was in my backpack in the backseat.

"Damn it!" America yelled from the top of the car. "I dropped my phone in the water!"

The faint rise and fall of tornado sirens blared in the distance as the hail was replaced by rain.

I reached back for my bag, slipped it over my shoulder, and climbed out of my window, joining America on top. Water was sloshing over the top of the hood. America crossed her bare arms over her chest, shivering in the wind, her hair already becoming saturated with rainwater. In just a pair of shorts, a tank top, and sandals, she was dressed for a hot summer day.

I took a quick look around, assessed the water, and then jumped off. It barely came to my waist.

"It's not deep, baby. Jump."

America squinted her eyes against the rain.

"We have to take shelter, America. Jump to me!"

She more fell than jumped, and then I helped her across the ditch to the grassy knoll. Cars were parked on both sides of the turnpike, but not all traffic was stopped. A semi blew past us, blowing America's hair back and soaking us with water.

America held out her arms at each side, her fingers sprawled out, her mascara running down her cheeks.

"I don't see anything, do you?" I asked.

She shook her head, using her tank top to wipe her face. "That doesn't mean anything though. They could have reports of circulation or lowering."

"That overpass is closer than town. Let's go there. We can call your parents ..."

A melody of screams echoed behind us, and I glanced back to see what was going on.

"Shepley!" America screamed, looking southwest in horror, toward the RV park nestled in a patch of trees. The branches were bending, nearly to their breaking point, thrashing helplessly in the raging wind.

"Fuck," I said, watching a cloud slowly fall from the sky.

America

Wet and freezing, I lifted my shaking hand to point toward the blue finger dangling from the clouds above. Someone shouldered past me, nearly knocking me forward, and I saw a man sprinting toward the overpass, hugging to him a toddler with pigtails and white sandals.

The turnpike led to an overpass over Highway 170. The RV park was below on one side, and a gas station was on the other side, just a quarter of a mile away.

Shepley held out his hand. "We should go."

"Where?"

"The overpass."

"If it goes over the bridge, we'll be sucked out," I said, my teeth beginning to chatter. I wasn't sure if it was because I was cold or terrified. "The gas station is the safest place!"

"It's closer than Emporia. Hopefully, it will miss us."

More people ran past us toward the junction, disappearing as they descended down the hill to hide under the bridge. A truck slammed on its brakes in the middle of the turnpike, and seconds later, an SUV rammed the truck. A loud crunching of metal and glass was muted from the growing wind created by the tornado. It had grown larger in just the few seconds when I turned away.

Shepley signaled for me to wait while he jogged to the wreckage. He peeked in, took a few steps back, and then rushed to check on the driver of the truck. His shoulders slumped. They were all gone.

"You can't stay here!" a woman said, tugging on my arm.

She held hands with a young boy, about ten years old. The whites of his eyes stood out against his dark bronze skin.

"Mom!" he said, pulling her away.

"It's going to plow straight through here! You have to find shelter!" the mother said again, taking off toward the gas station with her son.

Shepley returned to me, taking my hand. "We have to go," he said, turning to see dozens of people running toward us from their parked vehicles.

I nodded, and we began to run. The rain stung my face, blowing horizontally instead of toward the ground, making it hard to see.

Shepley looked back. "Go!" he said.

We ran across two lanes and then paused on the far side of the grass median. Traffic was light but still moving in both directions. We stopped for a moment, and then Shepley pulled me forward again, across both lanes of oncoming traffic and then down the on ramp toward the gas station. A tall sign overhead read *Flying J*. People were running from the parking lot toward the overpass.

Shepley stopped, and my chest was heaving.

"Where are you going?" Shepley asked no one in particular.

A man holding the hand of a grade school–aged girl ran past us, pointing ahead. "It's full! They can't fit any more!"

"Shit!" I cried. "Shit! What do we do?"

Shepley touched my cheek, worry tightening the skin around his eyes. "Pray it doesn't hit us."

We ran together to two bridges that allowed the turnpike passage over the top of Highway 170. Large concrete pillars loomed over us, creating the underbelly where the metal met the hillside. The crevices of both bridges were already pregnant with frightened people.

"There's no room," I said, feeling hopeless.

"We'll make room," Shepley said.

As we climbed the steep incline of the concrete hill, cars that were still crossing overhead sounded like bass drums. Parents had tucked their children into the deepest corners they could find and covered them with their own bodies. Couples huddled together, and a group of four teenage girls wiped their wet cheeks, alternating between cussing at their cell phones and praying.

"There," Shepley said, pulling me beneath the western bridge. "It's going to hit the east bridge first." He led me to the center where there was a small space just big enough for one of us. "Climb up, Mare," he said, pointing to the small lip preceding the two-feet deep concrete niche.

I shook my head. "There's no room for you."

He frowned. "America, we don't have time for this."

"It's coming!" someone from the west bridge cried.

Shepley grabbed each side of my face and planted a hard kiss on my lips. "I love you. We're going to be okay. I promise. Get up there."

He tried to guide me, but I resisted.

"Shep—" I said over the wind.

"Right now!" he demanded. He'd never spoken to me like that before.

I swallowed and then obeyed.

Shepley looked around, huffing and peeling his soaked T-shirt away from his torso. He noticed a man below holding up his cell phone.

"Tim! Get up here!" a woman called.

Tim slicked back his wet dark hair, continuing to point his phone in the direction of the tornado. "It's getting close!" he called back, smiling with excitement.

Children cried out, and a few adults did, too.

"Is this happening?" I said, feeling my heart thundering against my rib cage.

Shepley squeezed my hand. "Look at me, Mare. It'll be over soon."

I nodded quickly, leaning over to see Tim still filming. He took a step back and then began scrambling up the incline.

I pulled Shepley as close to me as I could, and he held me tight. Time seemed to pause. It was quiet—no wind, no crying, almost as if the whole world had held its breath in anticipation of the next few seconds. This was a moment in time that would change the lives of everyone who had taken cover under the wrong bridges.

Too quickly, peace was over, and the wind began to roar like a dozen military jets were slowly flying low overhead. The grass in the median below began to whip, and I felt like I was under a mile of water, the change in air pressure feeling heavy and disorienting. At first, I was pushed back a bit, and then I saw Tim being taken off his feet. He slammed to the ground, clawed at the concrete, and then grass before being sucked into the sky by an invisible monster.

Screams surrounded me, and my fingers dug into Shepley's back. He leaned toward me, but as the funnel made its way to the other side of the east bridge and then ours, the air changed. Another person cried as she lost her grip and was pulled out from our hiding place. One by one, anyone not tucked inside the nook where the hill met the bridge was ripped away.

"Hold on!" Shepley yelled, but his voice was snuffed out. He used every bit of his strength to push me further into the crevice.

I felt his body pulling away from me. His arms tightened around me, but when I began to scoot forward, he released me altogether and dug his toes into the concrete, leaning into the wind.

"Shep!" I yelled, watching as his fingers turned white, pressing against the ground.

He struggled for a moment to hand me his backpack.

I slid it over one arm and then reached out for him. "Take my hand!"

His feet began to slide, and he looked up at me, recognition and terror on his face. "Close your eyes, baby."

Once he said the words, he was gone, whipped out like he weighed nothing. I screamed his name, but my voice was lost in the deafening wind.

The air pressure changed, and the suction stopped. I ran down to the bottom, seeing a dark blue twisting rope barreling down the turnpike, tossing semis like they were toys. I crawled out, and then I ran from beneath the bridge, looking around in disbelief, feeling the sting of the rain on every inch of my exposed skin.

"Shepley!" I screamed, bending over. I held tight to his backpack, hugging it to me as if it were him.

The rain faded away, and I watched as the tornado grew in size, gracefully gliding toward Emporia.

I sprinted to the Charger, stopping at the top of the ditch. The turnpike was now a path of destruction with mangled cars and random pieces of debris lying everywhere. The wreckage from the semi and SUV were no longer there, a large piece of tin lying in its place.

Just moments before, Shepley and I had been on a road trip to see my parents. Now, I was in the middle of what looked like a war zone.

The water was still sloshing over the hood of the Charger.

"We were just in there," I whispered to no one. "He was just in there!" My chest heaved, but no matter how many breaths I took, I couldn't get enough air. My hands hit my knees, and then my knees hit the ground. A sob tore through my throat, and I wailed.

I hoped he would jog up to me and reassure me that he was okay. The longer I waited by the Charger without him, the more I panicked. He wasn't coming back. Maybe he was lying somewhere, hurt. I wasn't sure what to do. If I left to look for him, he might come to the Charger, but I wouldn't be there.

I sucked in a breath, wiping the rain and tears from my cheeks. "Please find your way back to me," I whispered.

Red and blue lights reflected off the wet asphalt, and I looked over my shoulder to see a police cruiser parked behind me. An officer hopped out and rushed around, kneeling next to me, and he placed a gentle hand on my back. *Reyes* was engraved on a bronze name badge pinned to his front shirt pocket. He tipped his blue felt hat, and the bronze star fastened to the front said *Kansas Highway Patrol.*

"Are you hurt?" Reyes reached out with his thick arms, wrapping a wool blanket around my shoulders.

I didn't realize how cold I'd been until the sweet relief of warmth sank into my skin.

The officer loomed over me, bigger than Travis. He took off his hat, revealing a clean-shaven scalp. His expression was severe, whether he meant for it to be or not. Two deep lines separated his bushy black eyebrows, and his eyes sharpened as he looked down upon me.

I shook my head.

"Is that your vehicle?"

"My boyfriend's. We took shelter beneath the overpass."

Reyes looked around. "Well, that was stupid. Where is he?"

"I don't know." When I said the words aloud, a new pain blazed through me, and I crumbled, barely catching myself as my palms flattened on the wet road.

"What's that?" he asked, pointing to the backpack in my arms.

"His ... it's his. He handed it to me before he ..."

A high-pitch chirp sounded, and then Reyes spoke, "Two-nineteen to Base H. Two-nineteen to Base G. Over."

"Two-nineteen, go ahead," a woman's voice said through the speaker. Her tone was flat, not at all overwhelmed.

"I've got a group of people who were taking shelter under the Highway Fifty and I Thirty-Five junction." He scanned the area, seeing injured people scattered up and down the turnpike. "The tornado passed through here. Ten-forty-nine to this location. We're going to need medical assistance. As many as they can spare."

"Copy that, two-nineteen. Ambulances are being dispatched to your location."

"Ten-four," Reyes said, returning his attention to me.

I shook my head. "I can't go anywhere. I have to look for him. He might be hurt."

"He might be. But you can't look for him until you get that taken care of." Reyes nodded toward my forearm.

A two-inch gash had opened my skin, and blood was mixing with rain, streaming crimson from the wound onto the asphalt.

"Oh, Jesus," I said, holding my arm. "I don't even know how that happened. But I ... I can't leave. He's out here somewhere."

"You're leaving. You can come back," Reyes said. "You can't help him right now."

"He'll come here. Back to the car."

Reyes nodded. "Is he a smart guy?"

"He's fucking brilliant."

Reyes managed a small smile. It softened his intimidating glare. "Then the hospital is the second place he'll look."

CHAPTER SEVEN

America

I TOUCHED THE BANDAGE ON MY ARM, the skin around it still pink and angry from being cleaned and stitched. I felt more comfortable in the pair of baby-blue scrubs the nurse had given me to change into than my wet and cold tank top and denim shorts. I had been sitting in the ER waiting room for an hour, still holding the Reyes' wool blanket, trying to think of how to tell Jack and Deana what had happened to their son—not that I could anyway. The phone lines were down.

The hospital had become a steady stream of the dead or dying, the wounded, and the lost. A dozen or more children had been brought in, covered in mud but otherwise without a scratch. From what I could tell, they'd been separated from their parents. Twice that number of parents had arrived, looking for their missing children.

The waiting room had been turned into a triage of sorts, and I ended up standing against the wall, unsure of what I was waiting for. A very round woman sat a few feet away, hugging four young children, all their faces smudged with dirt and tears. The woman wore a bright green shirt that said *Kids First Daycare* in childlike font. I shivered, knowing the children she was holding were only a precious few of those who'd been in her care.

My feet began to trudge toward the door, but a hand cupped my shoulder. For half a second, relief and overwhelming joy washed over me like a tidal wave. My eyes filled with tears before I even turned around. Even though Reyes was a welcome sight, the disappointment of him not being Shepley sent me over the edge.

I choked on a sob as my knees buckled, and Reyes helped me to the ground.

"Whoa!" he said. "Whoa, lady. Take it easy." His thick arms were as big as my head, and he had a permanent deep wrinkle between his brows. It was even deeper now as he watched my state of mind spiral.

"I thought you were him," I said once I had recuperated, if it were possible after being that devastated—again.

"Shepley?" he asked.

"Did you find him?"

Reyes hesitated, but then he shook his head. "Not yet. But I've found you twice, so I can find him once."

I wasn't sure if I could feel more hopeless. Emporia had been hit hard. An entire wall of the hospital had been ripped away, insulation and glass littering the ground. Cars in the parking lot were stacked on top of one another. One was sitting in the branches of a tree. Thousands of people were without power and running water, and they were the lucky ones. Hundreds were without homes, and dozens were missing.

Amid the devastation, I couldn't fathom where to begin to look for Shepley. I was on foot and had no supplies. He was out there somewhere, and he was waiting for me. I had to find him.

I stood up. Reyes helped.

"Take it slow," he said. "I'll try to find you a quiet place to wait for him."

"I've been waiting for an hour. The only reason he wouldn't have come to the car or here to find me is ..." I swallowed the pain, refusing to cry again. "What if he's hurt?"

"Ma'am"—he stepped into my path—"I can't let you—"

"America."

"Pardon?"

"My name. It's America. I know you're busy. I'm not asking for your help, but I am asking you to step out of my way."

He frowned. "You just got your arm sewed up, and you're going to hike out of town? It's going to be dark in a few hours."

"I'm a big girl."

"Not very smart though."

I craned my neck at him. "Here's your blanket."

"Keep it," he said.

I sidestepped, but he countered.

"Get out of my way, Reyes."

I tried to step around him, but he blocked me again, sighing.

"I'm getting ready to go back out on patrol. Give me five minutes, and you can ride along."

I looked at him in disbelief. "I can't ride along! I have to find Shepley!"

"I know," he said, looking around and gesturing for me to keep my voice down. "I'm going out that way. We'll both keep an eye out for him."

It took me a moment to reply. "Really?"

"But at dark ..."

"I understand," I said, nodding. "You can bring me back here."

"I'll ask around. There will be a Red Cross shelter. Maybe FEMA will be set up by then. You can't spend the night here. You'll never be able to sleep."

I couldn't smile, but I wanted to. "Thank you."

He fidgeted, uncomfortable with the appreciation. "Yeah. Cruiser's out this way," he said, gesturing to the parking lot.

I slid Shepley's backpack over my shoulders and then followed Reyes outside, under the stormy sky. My hair still damp, I twisted it and then knotted it into a bun, away from my face. My feet slid against the wet soles of my sandals, my toes already aching from the chilly air.

"Where are you from?" Reyes asked, pressing the keyless entry on his key ring.

We both settled into our seats. The fabric seats felt warm and soft.

"I grew up in Wichita, but I go to school in Eakins, Illinois."

"Oh, at Eastern State?"

I nodded.

"My brother went to school there. Small world."

"God, these seats are like memory foam and velvet." I sighed, leaning back.

Reyes made a face. "You've been uncomfortable for too long. They're more like toilet padding and tweed."

I breathed out a laugh through my nose, but I still couldn't form a smile.

His eyes softened. "We're going to find him, America."

"If he doesn't find me first."

Shepley

Rain spattered on my eyelids, tapping me awake. I blinked, covering my eyes with my hand, and my shoulder instantly complained … then my back … and then everything else. I pushed myself upright, finding myself sitting in a field of green plants. I guessed it was soybeans. Debris was all around me—everything from clothes to toys to pieces of wood. Fifty yards ahead, light glinted off the twisted metal of a bicycle. I grimaced.

My shoulder felt stiff as I tried to stretch it, and I growled when the sting turned into fire shooting through my arm. My once white T-shirt was soiled with mud mixed with crimson at the site of the pain.

I stretched the collar with my fingers to see a dirty mess of a laceration that spanned six inches from just above my heart to the edge of my left shoulder. When I moved, a foreign object moved with it, stabbing me from the inside. I touched the skin, sucking in air through my teeth. It hurt like a son of a bitch, but whatever had sliced open my skin was still in there.

With clenched teeth, I spread the skin with my fingers. I could see layers of skin and muscle and then something else, but it wasn't bone. It was a piece of brown wood, about an inch thick. Using my fingers like tweezers, I dug inside, crying out while fishing the huge splinter from my shoulder. The squishing sound of blood and tissue combined with the discomfort made my head swim, but an inch at a time, I extracted the stake and let it fall to the ground. I fell back, looking up at the weeping sky, waiting for the dizziness and nausea to subside, still trying to wade through my last memories.

My blood ran cold. *America.*

I scrambled to my feet, holding my left arm against my side. "Mare?" I screamed. "America!" I turned in a circle, looking for the turnpike, listening for tires humming along the asphalt.

Only the songs of birds and a slight breeze blowing along the soybean field could be heard.

Sunbeams cascaded from the sky to my right, helping me get my bearings. It was mid afternoon, meaning I was facing south. I had no idea which direction I'd been thrown.

I looked up, remembering my last words to America. I'd felt myself being pulled, and I hadn't wanted her to see it. I'd thought it would be the last thing I could protect her from. Then I had been launched into the air. The feeling had been hard to process, maybe something like skydiving but through a meteor shower. I had been pelted with what felt like tiny rocks, and in the next moment, a bicycle had rammed my legs and back. Then I had been slammed on the ground.

I blinked, feeling panic rise in my throat. The turnpike was either in front of me or behind me. I didn't know how to find myself, much less my girlfriend.

"America!" I yelled again, terrified she'd been sucked out as well.

She could be lying twenty feet from me or still tucked in the crevice at the overpass.

I decided to just walk south, hoping once I reached some sort of road, I'd be able to determine how far I was from the last place I'd seen my girlfriend. The soybeans grazed my wet jeans. My clothes were weighed down by the inch-thick layer of mud, and my shoes were like two blocks of concrete. My hair was caked in wet gravel and grime, and so was my face.

As I approached the edge of the field, I saw a large piece of tin with the words *Emporia Sand & Gravel.* As I crested a small hill, I saw the remains of the company, the piles of materials scattered from the wind—the same wind that had carried me at least a quarter of a mile from where I had taken shelter.

My feet slugged through the rain-soaked soil and sand, over the large pieces of wood frame and metal that had once been a large building. Trucks were overturned more than a hundred yards away.

I froze when I came upon a group of trees. A man was twisted in the branches, every orifice filled with pea gravel. I swallowed back the bile bubbling up in my throat. I reached up, barely able to touch the sole of his boot.

"Sir?" I said, barely able to speak above a whisper. I'd never seen anything so gruesome.

His foot swung, lifeless.

I covered my mouth and continued walking, calling out America's name. *She's okay. I know she is. She's waiting for me.* The words became a mantra, a prayer, as I crossed the countryside alone, trudging through the mud and grass, until I saw the red and blue flashes of an emergency vehicle.

With renewed energy, I ran toward the chaos, hoping to God I wouldn't just find America, but that I would also find her unscathed. She would be just as worried about me, so the urge to calm her fears was just as strong as the need to find her safe.

Three ambulances were parked along the turnpike, and I ran to the closest one, watching paramedics load up a young woman. Seeing that it wasn't America, relief washed over me.

The paramedic glanced at me and then did a double take, turning to me. "Whoa. Are you hurt?"

"My shoulder," I said. "I pulled a splinter out of it the size of a Sharpie."

I looked around while he assessed my wound.

"Yeah, that's going to need stitches. Probably staples. You definitely need to get it cleaned up."

I shook my head. "Have you seen a pretty blonde girl, early twenties, about this tall?" I asked, holding my hand up to my eye.

"I've seen a lot of blonde girls today, pal."

"She's not just a blonde girl. She's gorgeous, like epically beautiful."

He shrugged.

"Her name is America," I said.

He pressed his lips together in a hard line and then shook his head. "Girlfriend?"

"We slipped off the turnpike and went into a ditch. We took shelter under an overpass, but I'm not sure where I am."

"Vintage Charger?" he asked.

"Yeah?"

"Must have been that overpass," the paramedic said, nodding to the west. "Because your car is three hundred yards in that direction."

"Did you see a pretty blonde waiting close?"

He shook his head.

"Thanks," I said, heading toward the overpass.

"No one is over there. Everyone who took shelter at the overpass is either at the hospital or the Red Cross tent."

I slowly turned around, frustrated.

"You really need to get that cleaned out and sewn up, sir. And we still have weather coming in. Let me give you a ride to the hospital."

I looked around and then nodded. "Thanks."

"What's your name?" He closed the back doors and then knocked one door with the side of his fist twice.

The ambulance pulled forward and turned a one-eighty before heading toward Emporia with its lights and sirens on.

"Uh ... that was our ride."

"No, this is your ride," he said, showing me to a red-and-white SUV. The door read *Fire Chief.* "Get in."

When he climbed behind the wheel, he gave me a once-over. "You got carried off, didn't ya? How far do you think?"

I shrugged. "To the other side of that gravel plant. There was a body ... in the tree."

He frowned and then nodded. "I'll call it in. You were flung a little over a quarter of a mile, I bet. You're lucky you got away with just a scratch."

"It's a hell of a scratch," I said, instinctively stretching my shoulder until I felt a twinge.

"I agree," he said, slowing as we approached the Charger.

I stared at it as we passed, seeing that it was still submerged. America was gone.

My throat tightened. "If she's not at the overpass and she's not at the Charger, she went to the hospital."

"I agree with that, too," the Chief said.

"Hopefully, for shelter and not because she's hurt."

The Chief sighed. "You'll find out soon enough. First, you're going to get that wound cleaned."

"I don't have much daylight left."

"Well, you're definitely not going to find her at night."

"That's why I can't waste time."

"I'm not your dad, but I can tell you now, if infection sets in, you're not going to feel up to looking for her tomorrow. Get yourself taken care of, and then you can look for your girl."

I sighed and then pounded the door with the side of my fist. It was a lot harder than the Chief had hit on the ambulance door.

He shot me a side-eye.

"Sorry," I murmured.

"'S'all right. If it were my wife, I'd feel the same."

I peeked over at him. "Yeah?"

"Twenty-four years. Two grown girls. Are you going to marry this girl?"

I swallowed. "I had a ring in my bag."

He gave a half smile. "Where is it?"

"I handed it to her before I was blown out."

"Good thinking. She's holding on to it for safekeeping, and she doesn't even know. She'll get two good surprises when she sees you."

"I hope so, sir."

Chief made a face. "Hope? Where were you headed?"

"Her parents' house."

"She was introducing you to her parents? Sounds like your chances were pretty good."

"I've met her parents," I said, staring out the window. I was supposed to be going in the other direction with America, and instead, I was heading back to Emporia to find her. "Several times. And I've asked her to marry me—several times."

"Oh," Chief said. "You were going to ask her again?"

"I thought I'd try one last time."

"What if she says no?"

"I haven't decided. Maybe ask her why. Maybe ask her when. Maybe prepare myself for her leaving me one day."

"Maybe it's her turn to ask you."

My face screwed into disgust. "No." I laughed once. "She knows I wouldn't be happy about that. Things were good. Now, it doesn't really make sense that I was so upset. We were working toward it. We'd just moved in together. She was committed to me. She loves me. I made us both miserable over it."

Chief shook his head. "Shacked up, huh? That explains it. My wife always says to my daughters, 'Why buy the cow if you get the milk for free?' I bet she woulda said yes if you woulda made her wait to share your bed."

I breathed out a laugh. "Maybe. We practically lived together anyway. Either I was in her dorm room, or she was at my place."

"Or ... if she agreed to move in with you, it's possible she's just taking things at her own pace. She didn't say good-bye. She just said no."

"If she says no again, I'm pretty sure it's going to mean good-bye."

"Sometimes, good-bye is a second chance. Clears your head. Anyway ... missing someone makes you remember why you loved that person in the first place."

I choked and then tried to clear the emotion from my voice. I couldn't imagine walking away from America.

I wasn't just in love with her. It was like taking my first breath, then the second, and then every breath after that. America had come into my life, and then she was the reason for it.

"She's special, you know? She's a daddy's girl, but she'll tell you where to stick it if she doesn't like what you have to say. She'll slap a giant to protect the honor of her best friend. She hates good-byes. She wears this little gold cross around her neck and cusses like a sailor. She's my happily ever after."

"She sounds like a firecracker. Maybe she said no to make sure you're not going to leave at the slightest sign of rocky shores. I'm surrounded by girls, and I'll tell ya ... sometimes, they take shots at you to see if you'll run."

"I was fooling myself." My voice broke.

Chief got quiet. "I wouldn't say—"

"When I find her, I'm going to ask her. I'll ask her as many times as it takes, but just being with her is enough. I had to literally be ripped away from her to understand that."

Chief chuckled. "You wouldn't be the first man to need a knock on the noggin."

"I have to find her."

"You will."

"She's okay. Right?"

Chief looked over at me. I could see he didn't want to make a promise he couldn't keep, so he simply nodded, the wrinkles around his light eyes deepening.

"You'd better find a garden hose first, or she won't recognize you. You look like you lost a fight with a pottery wheel."

I laughed once. I tried to resist the urge to rub the dried mud from my face, not wanting to make a bigger mess in Chief's truck than I already had.

"You'll find her," Chief said. "And you'll marry her."

I offered an appreciative smile and then nodded once before turning to look out the window, searching the faces of everyone we passed on the way to the hospital.

CHAPTER EIGHT

America

REYES WAS TENDING TO A GRANDMOTHER and her teenage grandson who'd crawled out of the wreckage of their double-wide trailer home. Reyes had been patrolling up and down the highways and byways within a two-mile radius of where he'd picked me up, but we hadn't come across Shepley or anyone who had seen him. I was pissed that I didn't even have a picture of him. They were all on my phone, and my phone was drowning somewhere in the river. The battery had been in the single digits when I checked the weather, so it was probably dead.

Explaining what Shepley looked like was difficult. Short brown hair, hazel eyes, tall, good-looking, athletically built, six foot with no distinguishing marks made my description of him fairly vague even though he was anything but. For the first time, I wished he were a tattooed giant like Travis.

Travis. I bet he and Abby were so worried.

I returned to the cruiser and sat in the passenger seat.

"Any luck?" Reyes said.

I shook my head.

"Mrs. Tipton hasn't seen Shepley either."

"Thanks for asking. Are they okay?"

"A little banged up, but they'll live. Mrs. Tipton is missing her terrier, Boss Man." His words were hollow, but he wrote everything down on his clipboard.

"That's awful."

Reyes nodded, continuing his notes.

"All this going on, and you're going to help her find her dog?" I asked.

Reyes looked at me. "Her grandsons visit twice a year. That dog is the only thing between her and lonely. So, yeah, I'm going to help her. I can't do much, but I'll do what I can."

"That's nice of you."

"It's my job," he said, continuing his scribbling.

"Highway patrol helps with missing animals?"

He glared at me. "Today, I do."

I raised my chin, refusing to let his size and intimidating expression get to me. "Are you sure there's no way to get a call out?"

"I can take you back to headquarters."

I scanned the disaster that had been left of the trailer park. "After dark. We have to keep looking."

Reyes nodded, turning off his lights and pulling the gear into drive. "Yes, ma'am."

We pulled back onto the turnpike, and for the second time, Reyes drove toward the overpass to check with the emergency crew on the scene to see if they'd seen Shepley.

"Thank you again. For everything."

"How's your arm?" he asked, peeking over at my bandage.

"Sore."

"I can imagine."

"Do you have family here?" I asked.

"Yes, I do." His chiseled jaw danced under his skin, uncomfortable with the personal question.

He didn't seem to want to elaborate, so of course, I couldn't stop there.

"Are they okay?"

After a second of hesitation, he spoke, "Just missed them. Wife was a little shaken up."

"Them?"

"New little girl at home."

"How new?"

"Three weeks."

"I bet you were worried."

"Terrified," he said, staring forward. "I checked on them. A little roof damage. Hail damage on the new minivan."

"Oh, no. I'm sorry."

"It wasn't new. Just new to us. But nothing important."

"Good," I said. "I'm glad." I looked at the radio clock, feeling my eyebrows pulling in. "It's been two hours." I closed my eyes. "This trip was supposed to be *the* trip. I've been dropping hints left and right."

"For what?"

"For him to ask me ... to propose."

"Oh." He frowned. "How long have you been together?"

"Almost three years."

He puffed. "I asked Alexandra after three months."

"Did she say yes?"

He raised an eyebrow.

"I didn't," I said, picking dried mud off my hands. "He's asked me before."

"Ouch."

"Twice."

Reyes's entire face compressed. "Brutal."

"His cousin and my best friend are married. They eloped after a horrible accident at the college, and I—"

"The fire?"

"Yeah ... you've heard about it?"

"My brother's alma mater, remember?"

"Right."

"So, they got married? And it turned out bad?"

"No."

"But it was a deterrent to marry the guy you love?"

"Well, when you put it that way ..."

"How would you put it?"

"His roommate, Travis, got married. So, at first, he sort of proposed as an afterthought, hoping our parents would let us move in together. My parents weren't going for it ... at all. But I didn't want to get married just to manipulate a situation, like Travis and Abby. Travis is also his cousin, and Abby is my best friend." I glanced over at Reyes to see his expression. "I know. It's convoluted."

"Just a little."

"Then he asked me three months later, and I felt like he was just asking because Travis and Abby were married. Shep looks up to Travis. I just wasn't ready."

"Fair enough."

"Now," I let out a long sigh, "I'm ready, but he won't ask. He's talking about being a football scout."

"So?"

"So, he'll be gone for a good chunk of the year." I shook my head, picking at my dirty nails. "I'm afraid we'll grow apart."

"Scout, huh? Interesting." He shifted in his seat, preparing for what he would say next. "What's in the bag?"

I shrugged, looking down at the backpack in my lap. "His stuff."

"What kind of stuff?"

"I don't know. A toothbrush and a weekend's worth of clothes. We were going to visit my parents."

"You wanted him to propose at your parents' house?" Once again, his eyebrow arched.

I shot him a look. "So? This is starting to feel like less of a conversation and more of an interrogation."

"I'm curious why that bag is so important. It was the only thing besides you two to leave the car. He handed it to you before he was blown from the overpass. That's one important bag."

"What are you getting at?"

"I just want to make sure I'm not transporting drugs in my cruiser."

My mouth fell open and then snapped shut.

"Have I offended you?" Reyes asked although he was clearly unaffected by my reaction.

"Shepley doesn't do drugs. He barely drinks. He buys one beer and babysits it all night."

"What about you?"

"No!"

He wasn't convinced. "You don't have to do drugs to sell them. The best dealers don't."

"We're not drug dealers or smugglers or whatever the current term is."

Reyes pulled onto the shoulder beside the flooded Charger. Water and debris sloshed into the open windows. "That's going to cost a lot to repair. How is he going to pay for it?"

"He and his dad share a love for old cars."

"Restoration project for father-son bonding? All paid for with dad's money?"

"They didn't need to bond. He's very close with his parents. He was a good kid, and he's an even better man. Yes, they have money, but he has a job. He supports himself."

Reyes glared down at me. He was just ... massive. Still, I had nothing to hide, and I wouldn't let him intimidate me.

"He works at a bank," I snapped. "Do you really think I'm hiding drugs in this bag?"

"You've been holding on to it like it's made of gold."

"It's his! It's the only thing I have of him besides that drowned car!" Tears burned in my eyes as the realization of what I'd just said formed a lump in my throat.

Reyes waited.

I pressed my lips together and then tore at the zipper, yanking at it until it opened. I pulled out the first thing I grabbed, which was one of Shepley's shirts. It was his favorite, a dark gray Eastern State tee. I held it to my chest, instantly breaking down.

"America ... don't ... don't cry." Reyes looked half disgusted and half uncomfortable, trying to look anywhere else but me. "This is awkward."

I pulled out another shirt and then a pair of shorts. As I unrolled them, a small box fell back into the backpack.

"What was that?" Reyes said in an accusatory tone.

I dug in the bag and fished out the box, holding it up with a huge grin. "It's the ... this is the ring he bought. He brought it." I sucked in a ragged breath, my expression crumbling. "He was going to propose."

Reyes smiled. "Thank you."

"For what?" I said, opening the box.

"Not transporting drugs. I would have hated to arrest you."

"You're a jerk," I said, wiping my eyes.

"I know." He rolled down his window to flag down another officer.

With the help of the National Guard, the turnpike had been cleared, and traffic was running smoothly again, but as the sun began its descent, another set of dark clouds started to form on the horizon.

"That looks ominous," I said.

"I think we've already experienced ominous."

I frowned, feeling impatient. "We have to find Shepley before dark."

"Working on it." He nodded to an approaching officer. "Landers!"

"How's it going?" Landers said.

With him standing next to Reyes's window, even in a cruiser, I felt like we were being pulled over, and any minute, Landers would ask Reyes if he knew how fast he was going.

"I have a little girl in my car—"

"Little girl?" I hissed.

He sighed. "I have a young woman in my car who's looking for her boyfriend. They took shelter under that overpass when the tornado hit."

Landers leaned down, giving me a once-over. "She's lucky. Not all of them made it."

"Like who?" I asked, bending just enough to get a better look.

"I'm not sure. Can you believe one guy was thrown a quarter of a mile and ran all the way back to the turnpike, searching for someone? He was covered in mud. Looked like a melted candy bar."

"Was he alone? Do you remember his name?" I asked.

Landers shook his head, still chuckling at his own joke. "Something weird."

"Shepley?" Reyes asked.

"Maybe," Landers said.

"Was he hurt? What was he wearing? Early twenties? Hazel eyes?"

"Whoa, whoa, whoa, ma'am. It's been a long day," Landers said, standing up.

All I could see of him then was his midsection.

Reyes looked up at him. "C'mon, Justin. She's been looking for him for hours. She watched him get sucked out by a damn tornado."

"He had a significant laceration on his shoulder, but he'll live if the fire chief can talk him into getting it taken care of. He was hell-bent on finding his, um ... how did he put it? Epically beautiful girlfriend." Landers paused and then leaned down. "America?"

My eyes widened, and my mouth fell open into a gaping smile. "Yes! That's my name! He was here? Looking for me? Do you know where he went?"

"To the hospital ... to look for you," Landers said, tipping his hat. "Good luck, ma'am."

"Reyes!" I said, grabbing his arm.

He nodded once as he flipped on his lights, and then he threw the gear into drive. We bounced as the cruiser crossed the median, and then Reyes pressed a heavy foot on the gas, barreling down the turnpike toward Emporia ... and Shepley.

Shepley

The nurse shook her head, dabbing a cut on my ear with a cotton ball. "You're lucky." She blinked her long eyelashes and then reached behind her for something sitting on the silver tray next to my stretcher.

The ER was full. The rooms were only available for the more urgent cases. Triage had been set up in the waiting room, and I'd waited for over an hour before a nurse finally called my name and escorted me to a stretcher in the hall where I'd waited for another hour.

"I can't believe you were going to walk out of here."

"It's getting late. I have to find America before dark."

The nurse smiled. She was a tiny little thing. I'd thought she was fresh out of nursing school until she opened her mouth. She reminded me a lot of America—tough, confident, and would accept zero percent of shit anyone might give her.

"I told you. I looked," she said. "America is in the system, which means she's been seen here. She's probably out looking for you. Stay put. She'll come back."

I frowned. "That doesn't make me feel better"—I looked down at her badge—"Brandi."

She smirked. "No, but getting these wounds flushed will. Keep this clean and dry. You'll have a small nip gone from your ear."

"Fabulous," I murmured.

"You're the one who took shelter under an overpass. Don't you know anything? That's worse than standing in an open field. When a tornado goes over a bridge, it increases the wind velocity."

"Did they teach you that in nursing school?" I asked.

"This is Tornado Alley. If you don't know the rules already, you'll be eager to learn after the first tornado season."

"I can see why."

She breathed out a laugh. "Consider the ear bragging rights. Not many people can say they've taken a trip in a tornado and lived to tell about it."

"I don't think they'll be impressed by a chipped ear."

"If you're wishing for a gnarly scar, you'll have one," she said, pointing to my shoulder.

I looked down at the white bandage and tape on my shoulder and then behind me toward the door. "If she's not here in fifteen minutes, I'm going back out to look for her."

"I can't get your discharge papers ready in—"

"Fifteen minutes," I said.

She was unimpressed with my demand. "Listen, princess, if you haven't noticed, I'm busy. She'll be here. We've got another storm coming in anyway, and—"

I stiffened. "What? When?"

She shrugged, looking to the mounted television in the waiting room. People of all ages—all soaked with rainwater, filthy, and scared—stood, wrapped in hospital-issued wool blankets. They began to crowd around the screen. A meteorologist was standing in front of a radar moving a few inches at a time. A large red blob surrounded by yellows and greens crept up to Emporia's city limits, and then it started over, stuck in a loop.

"It's going to swallow us up and spit us out," Brandi said.

My eyebrows pulled in as the panic swelled in my chest. "She's still out there. I don't even know where to look."

"Shepley," Brandi said, grabbing my chin and forcing me to face her, "stay put. If she comes back here and finds out you've left, what do you think she's going to do?" When I didn't answer, she let go of my chin, disgusted. "Do the same thing you would. Go looking for you. This is the safest place for her, and if you stay here, she'll find her way back."

I gripped the edge of the stretcher, squeezing the plastic-covered cushion in my fist, while Brandi carefully slid a scrub top over my head. She helped me slip my arms through, patiently waiting, while I struggled with lifting my left shoulder.

"I can get you a hospital gown instead," she said.

"No. No gowns," I said. Grunting, I maneuvered my arm through the sleeve.

"You can't even get dressed, but you're going to go look for her?"

"I can't just sit here, safe and warm, while America's out there somewhere," I said. "She probably has no clue she's about to get hit again with more weather."

"Shepley, listen to me. We're still under a tornado warning."

"It's impossible to get hit twice in the same night."

"Actually, it's not," she said. "It's rare, but it happens."

I climbed off the stretcher, my breath catching when the torn muscle in my arm moved.

"Fine. If you're gonna insist on being ridiculous, you have to sign an AMA."

"Sign a what?"

"AMA—Against Medical Advice."

"Whoa, whoa, whoa," Chief said, holding up his hands. "Where do you think you're going?"

I breathed out through my nose, frustrated. "Another storm is coming in. She's not back yet."

"That doesn't mean it's a good idea for you to head out into the rain."

"What if it were your wife, Chief? What if your daughters were out there? Would you go?"

Tornado sirens filled the air. They were much louder this time, the eerie drone sounding like it was just outside the doors. Everyone looked around, and then the panic began.

I started for the door.

But Chief stood in front of me. "You can't go out there, Shepley! It's not safe!"

Holding my left arm to my middle, I shouldered past him and then pushed my way through the crowded waiting room to the doors. The sky had opened up again, pouring down rain on the parking lot. With horror and disbelief on their faces, people were running across the cement to the emergency room.

I looked up for signs of a funnel cloud. I had no car and no idea where she was. I'd been afraid plenty of times in my life, but none of them had ever come close to this. Keeping the ones you love safe wasn't a question, but I couldn't save her.

I turned around, grabbing Chief's shirt with my fist, his badge digging into my palm. "Help me," I said, shaking with fear and frustration.

Screams erupted, and power flashes sparked in the distance.

"Everyone, get in the hallways!" Chief said, yanking me back to my stretcher.

I fought him, but even though he was twice my age, with the use of both of his arms, he easily overpowered me.

"Get! Your Ass! Down!" he growled, struggling to push me toward the floor.

Brandi put a young boy in my lap and held on to three more children, hunkering down next to me.

The young boy didn't cry, but he shook uncontrollably. I blinked and looked around, seeing the terror-filled faces of everyone around us. Most of them had already suffered through one devastating tornado.

"I want my dad," the young boy in my lap whimpered.

I hugged him to my side, trying to shield as much of his body as I could. "It's going to be okay. What's your name?"

"I want my dad," he said again, on the edge of panic.

"My name is Shep. I'm alone, too. You think you could hang out here with me until this is over?"

He looked up at me with big russet eyes. "Jack."

"Your name is Jack?" I asked.

He nodded.

"That's my dad's name," I said with a small smile.

Jack mirrored my expression, and then his grin slowly vanished. "It's my dad's name, too."

"Where is he?" I asked.

"We were in the bathtub. My mom … my baby sister. It got real loud. My dad held on to me tight. Real tight. When it was over, he wasn't holding me anymore. Our couch was upside down, and I was under it. I don't know where he is. I don't know where any of them are."

"Don't worry," I said. "They'll know to look for you here."

Something slammed into a pane window and shattered the glass. Frightened cries barely registered over the sirens and blustering wind.

Jack buried his head into my chest, and I gently squeezed him with my good arm, holding my left against my middle.

"Where's your family?" Jack asked, his eyes clenched.

"Not here," I said, peeking over my shoulder at the broken window.

CHAPTER NINE

America

"HOW MUCH FARTHER?" I asked.

"Two miles less than the last time you asked," Reyes grumbled.

Reyes was driving fast but not fast enough. Just knowing that Shepley was at the hospital, hurt, made me feel like I could jump out of the car and run faster than what we were going. We had exited off the turnpike to a road with a narrow stretch of houses that had somehow been missed by the tornado.

I'd rolled down the window, and I was resting my chin on my hand, letting the air blow against my face. I closed my eyes, imagining the look on Shepley's face when I walked through the door.

"Landers said he was pretty beat up. You should prepare yourself for that," Reyes said.

"He's okay. That's all I care about."

"Just don't want you to be upset."

"Why?" I turned to him. "I thought you were the badass trooper with no emotions."

"I am," he said, squirming in his seat. "Doesn't mean I want to see you cry again."

"Doesn't your wife cry?"

"No," he said without hesitation.

"Ever?"

"I don't give her a reason to."

I sat back in my seat. "I bet she cries. She probably just doesn't show it. Everybody cries."

"I've never seen her cry. She laughed a lot when Maya was born."

I smiled. "Maya. That's cute."

Huge drops of rain began to spatter on the windshield, prompting Reyes to switch on the wipers. The back and forth and drag across the glass began a cadence that echoed every beat of my heart.

One corner of his mouth turned up. "She is cute. Head full of black hair. She came out, looking like she was wearing a toupee. She was bright yellow the first week. I thought she just had a naturally great tan ... like me." He smirked. "But it turned out to be jaundice. We took her to the doctor and then the lab. They stabbed her heel with a needle and squeezed her foot for a blood sample. Alexandra didn't shed a tear. I cried as much as Maya did. You think I'm tough? You haven't met my wife."

"Your wedding day?"

"Nope."

"When she found out she was pregnant?"

"Nope."

I thought about it for a while. "Not even happy tears?"

He shook his head.

"What about the women you pull over? Do you let them go if they tear up?"

"It makes me uncomfortable," he said simply. "I don't like it."

"Good thing you married a woman who doesn't cry."

"Lucky. Very, *very* lucky. She's not overly emotional."

"Doesn't sound like she's emotional at all," I teased.

"You're not far off." He laughed once. "I wasn't sure she even liked me at first. It took me two years and a lot of hours at the gym to even get up the nerve to ask her out. I didn't think I could love anyone more than I loved Alexandra until a few weeks ago."

"When Maya was born?"

He nodded.

I smiled. "I was wrong. You're not a jerk."

A shrill tone came over the radio, and the dispatcher began rattling off a weather report.

"Another tornado?" I asked.

Then the sirens began to wail.

"The National Weather Service is reporting a tornado on the ground within Emporia city limits," the dispatcher said in a monotone voice. "All units be advised, a tornado is on the ground."

"How is she so calm?" I asked, looking up at the sky.

Dark clouds were swirling above us.

Reyes slowed, looking up. "That's Delores. It's her job to be calm, but also, nothing rattles that woman. She's been doing this since before I was born."

Delores's voice came over the radio again. "All units be advised, a tornado is on the ground, traveling north, northeast. Current location is Prairie Street and South Avenue."

Delores continued to repeat the report while Reyes's eyebrows pulled together, and he began frantically searching the sky.

"What's wrong?" I asked.

"We're a block north of that location."

Shepley

The wind blew in clusters of rain, soaking the tile and toppling chairs. Several men with hospital badges rushed over with a large piece of plywood, hammers, and nails, and then they got to work covering the broken glass. A few more swept up the glistening pieces of glass that had scattered onto the floor.

Chief stood and started to walk over to where the maintenance men worked. Just as he began to chat with one of the men, he glanced out the window. Then he turned on his heels and yelled, "Everybody, move!"

He grabbed a woman and leaped just as a compact car punched through the plywood and the remaining windows, coming to a halt on its side in the middle of the waiting room.

After a few seconds of stunned silence, wailing and yelling filled the room. Brandi turned the children she'd been holding over to me, and she ran over to the car, checking the workers and some patients who had been mowed down.

She held her palm on the forehead of a man, blood gushing down his face. "I need a stretcher!"

Chief stirred and then looked up at me with confused eyes.

"You all right?" I asked, hugging the children around me.

He nodded and then helped up the woman he'd pushed out of the way.

"Thank you," she said, looking around in a daze.

Chief peeked out the hole in the wall that the car had created. "It's passed."

He took a step toward the broken bodies around the car but paused when his radio came on.

A deep voice broke through as a man spoke, "Two-nineteen to Base G."

"Base G. Go ahead," the dispatcher spoke back.

Chief turned up his radio. He could hear the disguised panic in the officer's voice.

"Officer down at Highway Fifty and Sherman. My cruiser has been overturned. Multiple fatalities and injuries in this area, including me. Requesting ten-forty-nine to this location. Over," he said, grunting the last word.

"How badly are you injured, Reyes?" the dispatcher said.

Chief glanced up at me. "I have to go."

"Not sure," the officer said. "I was bringing a young woman to the hospital. She's unconscious. I think her leg is trapped. We're going to need some hardware. Over."

"Copy that, two-nineteen."

"Delores?" Reyes said. "Her boyfriend was reported to be at Newman Regional with the fire chief. Can you radio the hospital to notify?"

"Ten-four, Reyes. You hang in there. We have units on the way."

I gripped Chief's arm. "That's her. America is with that cop."

"Base G is the Turnpike Highway Patrol. She's with a state trooper."

"It doesn't matter who she's with. He's hurt, and she's stuck in there. He can't help her."

Chief turned away from me, but I tightened my grip on his arm.

"Please," I said. "Take me there."

Chief made a face, already against the idea. "By the sounds of it, they're going to have to cut her out of the cruiser. That could take hours. She's unconscious. She won't even know you're there, and you'll probably just get in the way."

I swallowed and looked around as I thought. Chief pulled his keys out of his pocket.

"Just …" I sighed. "You don't have to take me. Just tell me where it is, and I'll walk."

"You'll walk?" Chief said in disbelief. "It's dark. No electricity means no streetlights. No moon because of the clouds."

"I have to do something!" I yelled.

"I'm the fire chief. There's an officer down. I'm going to oversee the extraction and—"

"I'm begging you," I said, too tired to fight. "I can't stay here. She's unconscious, she might be hurt, and she'll be scared when she wakes up. I have to be there."

Chief thought about it for a few seconds and then sighed. "All right. But stay out of the goddamn way."

I nodded once, following when he turned for the parking lot. It was still raining, making me worry about her even more. What if the car was overturned in a drainage ditch, like the Charger? What if she was under water?

Chief turned on the lights and sirens as he navigated the SUV out of the hospital parking lot. Downed electrical lines and branches were everywhere, as were beaten vehicles of all shapes and sizes. Even a boat was lying on its side in the middle of the street. Families were making their way to the hospital on foot, and city workers were in high gear, trying to remove the debris to the entrance road of the hospital.

"Dear God," Chief whispered, staring at our surroundings in awe. "Hit twice in the same day. Who would have ever thought?"

"Not me," I said. "I'm looking right at it, and I still don't believe it."

Chief turned south, heading toward Reyes and America.

"How far is it—where Reyes said they were?"

"Six blocks maybe. I'm not sure if we'll be the first ones on the scene or not, but—"

"We're not," I said, already seeing the flashing lights.

Chief drove a few more blocks and then pulled to the side of the road. First responders were already blocking the road, and firefighters were crowding the overturned cruiser.

I ran over to the vehicle. I was stopped at first until Chief gave the word. I fell on my knees, next to a paramedic beside the cruiser. Surrounded by debris, the vehicle was mashed in spots, every window shattered.

"Mare?" I cried, pressing my face against the wet dirt.

Half of the car was still in the street, and the other half—America's side—had settled on the grass.

Blonde waves snaked out of the small opening that was once the passenger window. The long tendrils were soaked with rain, pink in a small section.

My breath caught, and I looked over my shoulder to the paramedic. "She's bleeding!"

"We're working on it. You're going to have to move in a second, so I can start her a line."

I nodded. "Mare?" I said again, reaching in.

I wasn't sure what I was touching, but I could feel her soft skin. She was still warm.

"Be careful!" the medic said.

"America? Can you hear me? It's Shep. I'm here."

"Shepley?" a small voice called from the vehicle.

The paramedic pushed me out of the way. "She's awake!" he yelled to his partner.

The activity of emergency personnel around the car increased.

"Shepley?" America called, this time louder.

An officer picked me up off the ground and held me back.

"I'm here!" I called.

A small hand reached out into the rain, and I fell on my knees, crawling toward her.

I grabbed her hand before anyone could stop me. "I'm here, baby. I'm right here." I kissed her hand, feeling something sharp on my lips.

On her ring finger was the diamond I had planned to propose to her with—again—this weekend at her parents' house.

My bottom lip trembled, and I kissed her fingers again. "Stay awake, Mare. They're going to get you out of there soon."

I lay on the ground, holding her hand, for a few minutes until a firefighter brought over a hydraulic tool to pry open the door. The officer pulled me out of the way, and America reached for me with her fingers again.

"Shepley?" she cried.

"He's going to stand back a bit while we get you out of there, okay? Sit tight, ma'am."

The same officer from before patted my shoulder. It was then that I noticed he had bandages on his head.

"You're Reyes?" I asked.

"I'm sorry, sir. I tried to get us out of the way. It was too late."

I nodded once.

Chief approached. "You should let me take you to the hospital, Reyes."

"Not until she's out," he said, staring at the firefighters positing the tool.

With a single handle, the firefighter positioned two metal pincers near the door. The high-pitched whine of the hydraulics melded with the loud drone of the fire trucks.

America cried out, and I lunged toward the cruiser.

Reyes held on to me. "Stand back, Shepley," he said. "They'll get her out faster if you stay out of the way."

My jaw clenched tight. "I'm right here!" I called.

The sun had set, and floodlights had been positioned all around the cruiser. Covered bodies were lying in a line along the sidewalk, barely one hundred yards away. It was almost impossible to stand there and wait for someone else to help America, but there was nothing I could do but let her know that I was still close. Waiting for them to free her was the only option.

I covered my mouth with my hand, feeling tears burning my eyes. "How long?" I asked.

"Just a few minutes," Chief said. "Maybe less."

I watched them cut and pry the door off the cruiser, and then they worked to free her leg. She cried out again. Reyes's grip on my arm grew tighter.

"She is a firecracker," he said. "She wouldn't take no for an answer. Insisted on riding with me, hoping she would find you."

Chief laughed once. "I know someone like that."

The paramedic reached in with a neck collar, and once he stabilized her neck, he pulled her out, inch by inch. Once I saw her face and her beautiful big eyes looking around in shock and awe, the tears fell.

I stood a few feet away while they stabilized her on the stretcher, and then I was finally allowed to hold her hand again.

"She's going to be okay," the paramedic said. "She's got a small cut on the crown of her head. Her left ankle is likely broken. That's the worst of it."

I looked down at America and kissed her cheek, feeling relief wash over me. "You found the ring."

She smiled, a tear falling from the corner of her eye and down her temple. "I found the ring."

I swallowed. "I know it's a traumatic situation. I know that you hate that Abby asked Travis after the fire, but—"

"Yes," America said without hesitation. "If you're asking me to marry you, yes." She sucked in a breath, tears streaming from her eyes.

"I'm asking you to marry me," I choked out before kissing the ring on her finger.

Once the paramedics loaded America's stretcher into the ambulance, I followed Reyes into the back with her. She winced when we went over bumps, but she never let go of my hand.

"I can't believe you're here," she said softly. "I can't believe you're okay."

"I never stay lost for long. I can always find my way back to you."

America breathed out a small laugh and closed her eyes, letting herself relax.

CHAPTER TEN

America

"It's beautiful," I said, looking around Travis and Abby's new home. "Did you say four bedrooms?"

Abby nodded. "Two downstairs, two up."

I lifted my chin, looking up the stairs. They were lined by white wooden spindles and covered by newly laid taupe carpet. The wood floors were sparkling, and the new furniture, rugs, and décor had been placed perfectly.

"It looks like it's straight from *Better Homes and Gardens* magazine," I said, shaking my head in awe.

Abby looked around with a smile, sighing and nodding. "We've been saving for a long time. I wanted it to be perfect. So did Trav."

I twirled my wedding ring around my finger. "It is. You look tired."

"Unpacking and organizing will do that to you," she said, walking into the living room.

She sat on the ottoman, and I sat on the sofa. It was the second thing Travis had purchased since he'd met Abby.

"He's going to love it when he gets home," I said. "They should be here soon."

She looked at her watch, absently twisting a long caramel strand. "Any minute actually. Remind me to thank Shepley for picking him up from the airport. I know he doesn't like to leave you alone these days."

I looked down, running my palm over my round belly. "You know he'd do anything for you and Travis."

Abby rested her chin on her fist and shook her head. "It's hard to believe yours will be Jim's fourth grandbaby. Olive, Hollis, Hadley, and now …"

"Still not telling," I said with a smile.

"C'mon! It's killing me not to know! Just tell me the gender."

I shook my head, and Abby laughed, only half-frustrated with my secret.

"It's still our secret—at least for three more weeks."

Abby grew quiet. "Are you afraid?"

I shook my head. "Looking forward to not being a waddling puffy incubator, to be honest."

Abby tilted her head, sympathetic. She reached over to the end table to straighten a frame that held a black-and-white photo from their vow renewal in St. Thomas.

I touched my belly, pressing in on whatever baby part was stretching against my ribs. "In about six months, you're going to have to move your breakables to higher ground."

Abby grinned. "Looking forward to it."

The front door opened, and Travis yelled across the foyer, his voice carrying easily into the living room, "I'm home, Pigeon!"

"I'll let you guys catch up," I said, positioning myself to scoot off the sofa.

"No, stay," Abby said, standing.

"But … he's been gone for ten days," I said, watching her saunter across the room to meet Travis in the wide doorway.

"Hi, baby," Travis said, slipping both arms around his wife. He pressed his lips against hers, breathing her in through his nose.

Shepley sat on the sofa next to me, kissing me and then my belly. "Daddy's here," he said.

The baby shifted, and I sat up, trying to allow for more space.

"Somebody missed you," I said, running my fingers over Shepley's hair.

"How are you feeling?" he asked.

"Good," I said, nodding.

He frowned. "I'm getting impatient."

I arched an eyebrow. "You are?"

He laughed once and then looked up at his cousin.

"Where you goin'?" Travis asked, watching Abby leave for the kitchen. She came back with two helium balloons on a string and a shoebox. He chuckled, confused, and then read the top of the box. "Welcome home, Daddy."

"Oh my *God*!" I screamed before covering my mouth.

Holding the box, Travis looked at me, then Shepley, and then back at Abby. "It's cute. Is it for Shep?"

Abby slowly shook her head.

Travis swallowed, his eyes instantly glossing over. "For me?"

She nodded.

"You're pregnant?"

She nodded again.

"I'm going to be a dad?" He looked at Shepley, his eyes wide, a huge goofy grin on his face. "I'm going to be a dad! No fuckin' way! No way!" he said, a tear falling down his face. He laughed, a bordering-on-crazy high-pitched laugh.

He wiped his cheek and then took Abby in his arms, whirling her around. Abby giggled, burying her face in his neck.

He set her down. "Really?" he asked, cautious.

"Yes, baby. I wouldn't joke about this."

He laughed again, relieved. I'd never seen Travis so happy.

"Congratulations," Shepley said, standing.

He walked over to Travis and hugged him. Travis grabbed him, obviously crying.

Abby wiped her eyes, just as surprised as the rest of us at Travis's reaction. "There's more," she said.

Travis let go of Shepley. "More? Is everything okay?" he asked with red blotches around his eyes.

"Open the box," Abby said, pointing to the shoebox still in Travis's hand.

He blinked a few times and then looked down, carefully tearing the brown paper it was wrapped in. He lifted the lid and then looked up at Abby. "Pidge," he breathed.

"What? Show me! I can't move!" I said.

Travis pulled out two tiny pairs of gray linen baby shoes, pinched between all four fingers.

I covered my mouth again. "Two?" I shrieked. "Twins!"

"Holy shit, brother," Shepley said, patting Travis's back. "Way to go."

Travis choked, overwhelmed with emotions. Once words came to him, he guided Abby to his recliner. "Sit, baby. Rest. This house looks amazing. You've worked hard." He knelt in front of her. "Are you hungry? I can cook you something. Anything. Name it."

Abby laughed.

"You're making me look bad, Trav," Shepley teased.

"Like you haven't made a huge fuss over me this entire time," I said.

Shepley sat next to me, hugging me to his side and kissing my temple.

"Grandbaby number five … and six," I said, beaming.

"I can't wait to tell Dad," Travis said. His bottom lip quivered, and he pressed his forehead against her belly.

"This ragtag family has done okay," Shepley said, touching my belly.

"We've done fucking amazing," Travis said.

Shepley stood, disappeared into the kitchen, and then returned with two open beer bottles and two bottles of water. He handed a beer to Travis and then the waters to Abby and me. We held up our drinks.

"To the next generation of Maddoxes," Shepley said.

Travis's dimple sank in when he smiled. "May their lives be as beautiful as the women who carried them."

I lifted my water. "You've always been good at toasts, Trav."

We all took a sip, and then I watched as Travis, Shepley, and Abby laughed and chatted about how amazing life had become, our impending parentage, and what life would be like from now on.

Travis couldn't stop smiling, and Abby seemed to be falling in love with him all over again while watching him fall in love with the idea of being a father.

For people who had struggled for every step forward, we didn't have one regret, and we wouldn't change a thing. Every wrong turn had led us to this moment, proving that every choice we'd made was right. We had cried and hurt and bled our way to happiness, the kind that couldn't be stopped by fire or wind.

However it had happened and whatever it was, we were something beautiful.

THE END.

ACKNOWLEDGMENTS

Something Beautiful is my seventeenth published work. Just six years ago, I sat down to write *Providence*, and life is so different in the most wonderful way. The overwhelming support and loyalty of my readers have played a major part in allowing me to write seventeen novels and novellas in six years, and for that, you have my sincere thanks.

Thank you to my dear friend Deanna Pyles, who helped me mold *Something Beautiful* from page one. You'll never know how much I appreciate your excitement and enthusiasm.

A special thank you to Sarah Hansen, Murphy Hopkins, Elaine Hudson York, and Kelli Spear for helping me package the *Something Beautiful* ARC in time for Vegas. I was certain my last-minute idea was going to fall apart, but you dropped what you were doing and worked late hours under tremendous pressure to make it happen. You made one hundred readers very happy. Thank you is not enough!

As always, thank you to my husband and children for your endless patience and support. It's not as easy as it sounds to have a wife and mom who works at home, but you have to pretend she's not there. We've perfected our process, and I love you more than words can say for rolling with my strange schedule. I couldn't do this without you guys. I wouldn't want to.

ABOUT THE AUTHOR

JAMIE MCGUIRE was born in Tulsa, Oklahoma. She attended Northern Oklahoma College, the University of Central Oklahoma, and Autry Technology Center where she graduated with a degree in Radiography.

Jamie paved the way for the New Adult genre with the international bestseller *Beautiful Disaster*. Her follow-up novel, *Walking Disaster*, debuted at #1 on the *New York Times*, *USA Today*, and *Wall Street Journal* bestseller lists. *Beautiful Oblivion*, book one of the Maddox Brothers series, also topped the *New York Times* bestseller list, debuting at #1. In 2015, books two and three of the Maddox Brothers series, *Beautiful Redemption* and *Beautiful Sacrifice*, respectively, also topped the *New York Times*.

Novels also written by Jamie McGuire include: apocalyptic thriller and 2014 UtopYA Best Dystopian Book of the Year, *Red Hill*; the Providence series, a young adult paranormal romance trilogy; *Apolonia*, a dark sci-fi romance; and several novellas, including *A Beautiful Wedding*, *Among Monsters*, *Happenstance: A Novella Series*, and *Sins of the Innocent*.

Jamie lives in Steamboat Springs, Colorado, with her husband, Jeff, and their three children.

Find Jamie at www.jamiemcguire.com or on Facebook, Twitter, Tsu, and Instagram.

CPSIA information can be obtained
at www.ICGtesting.com
Printed in the USA
LVOW03s1618041017
550621LV00001B/5/P